THE
PEGASUS
ADVENTURE

J.P. STANIFORTH

THE
PEGASUS
ADVENTURE

MEREO
Cirencester

Published by Mereo

Mereo is an imprint of Memoirs Publishing

25 Market Place, Cirencester, Gloucestershire GL7 2NX
Tel: 01285 640485, Email: info@mereobooks.com
www.memoirspublishing.com, www.mereobooks.com

ISBN: 978-1-909544-85-7

Book jacket design Ray Lipscombe

Printed in England

FOREWORD

I have read this novel with great interest and have to say it is exactly the kind of imaginative futuristic novel that I enjoy. I like the author's narrative style, too, which gives impetus to the story. The gift of telling a story is a unique gift, and this novel appears to have all the right ingredients—the vivid opening with ships travelling against the black backdrop of space, human engineering, cryogenics, anti-grav devices, the supply of android females, you name it!

The author envisages a future that is quite feasible, if one considers the totalitarian political forces at work today that threaten to engulf our planet in one form of dictatorship or another—a New World Order where the individual loses his freedom of choice and freedom of speech. To ensure that no-one can escape this monopoly of government, even space travel has been forbidden—or, indeed, any venture into space. In reaction to this, a small band of adventurous people, mainly scientists, have come together to plan and work together to elude the throttlehold of a world dictatorship—in an isolated place, a desert no less, surprisingly, in a remote area of China! Secrecy, of course, is of the utmost importance. Will they succeed in building a spacecraft that will take them outside the earth's atmosphere—and propel them to a new life of freedom and adventure, to a new world that they can seed to form a new earth where there are new heavens and new untethered ideologies?

The book is a page-turner, not just on account of the impetus of the story, but because of the fascinating, yet believable technological innovations that emerge as a result of the lateral and collaborative thinking of the individuals concerned. If you like innovative and inspired SF, then you will certainly love this adventure which so appropriately bears the name of Pegasus, the mythological winged divine source of inspiration.

Charles H. Muller
MA (Wales), PhD (Lond), DEd (SA), DLitt (UOFS)

CHAPTER ONE

———◆———

The vast and lonely blackness of space was encroached by a minute, unnaturally smooth body. This phenomenon laboriously inched its way across the frigid firmament with a peculiar visibility, a tell-tale trail of ionised particles which issued from an aperture on one of the convex surfaces of this peculiar circular shaped body. It stood out clearly against the background of stars, meteorites and debris which formed the cosmic norm. The trail twinkled and glowed as fireflies did on the world from which it came. The trail indicated the direction that had been travelled recently. Within a relatively short space of time the interstellar wind would sweep up the few remnants, absorbing them into the all-embracing dust of ages.

An observer might also have witnessed a second somewhat larger body, which followed relentlessly. The second speck emitted no trail of sparkling incandescence and only stood out from the background of fiery stars and dull planetoids because, like the first one, its movement was at an oblique angle to the common plane of circulation of the constellation through which both were passing.

This unwelcome and entirely unexpected chase was causing consternation on board the vessel, which left behind such evidence of its unnatural nature. Inside the vessel a humanoid figure was urgently searching memory banks for any explanation that may provide a clue to how to deal with this unexpected development. The frantic search caused no outward show on the face of the figure which remained quietly standing alongside the manual controls in the shallow depression in the panelling that was as much comfort as was required by an android. The terminals at the base of the neck gave adequate communication with the authoritative on-board D.R.A.K. to allow complete integration with the miniature internal version within the android's chest. The search was useless. No earthbound rational consciousness had foreseen the present circumstances; the android made the first move from the position she had adopted over one hundred years previously.

The override circuit was made:

Roland Stern slowly opened his eyes, blinked, and closed them again; the saline solution, which covered him, stung slightly...

I was confused, what was happening? I lay quite still for several minutes, then my brain gradually started to function. I remembered the take-off celebrations. President Ho Chek and other Earth Confederation bigwigs, in fulsome praise for us on the eve of our departure. I smiled to myself as the old-fashioned term bigwigs came to mind; I wondered how such a phrase had worked its way into my first thoughts at this time. The last thought gave me a jolt: where were we?

I tried moving again. As I opened my eyes once more, the slight sting of the warm fluid over my eyeballs, the fluid which was so essential to revive frozen tissues in the rapid transition from the recent state of cryo-hibernation.

Gradually my thoughts became clearer; the brain began

to perform more normally. I was breathing through my mouth; now I could feel the mouthpiece; my jaws were aching slightly. I clenched and unclenched my hands, turned my head first left then right. Slowly the training brief oscillated back, replacing more immediate fantasies. I felt for the lever by my right hand; this opened the drain valve of this coffin-like transportation module. As the liquid retreated I envisaged the ship's cabin automatically pressurising. This would enable me to remove the mouthpiece connected to the personal air supply. I waited patiently for the lid of my container to open.

It would take several minutes for the cabin to warm up and I had no intention of leaving this snug cocoon naked as a newborn infant until sure of the outside temperature. Eventually the lid swung open. I again waited for the next stage; the casket methodically rotated into an upright position and I stepped out into the enfolding comfort of the large soft towel that the android held ready.

Anthea helped me to dry my weary body. (How long had I been at rest?) Then, quickly into disposable briefs followed by a standard issue thermo-suit. The suit was command colour, red with three gold stars emblazoned on each shoulder to denote executive commander.

The commander was responsible for all actions now that we had left earth and therefore must be the first person to be aroused when we reach our destination, or as now, if some unexpected problem arose.

I was not left long in doubt.

Soon I was dressed; Anthea offered a quick gulp of Nerfi, a drink of concentrated glucose laced with a derivative of the traditional drug caffeine. I grimaced as I felt something not unlike a kick in the stomach, then almost immediately a gratifying glow all over. In a few seconds my mind became crystal clear. I looked around, noting that Anthea was already logging the dose in my personal medical file.

I moved to the duty officer control position, magnetic soles ringing noisily on the deck plates. The headset was waiting. I slipped it on, the single earpiece fitting itself comfortably to my left ear; immediately I started to assimilate the stream of data. Meanwhile, my eyes clear and bright now, were reading the multitude of dials and indicators that ranged before me. These were set out in ten panels, each with its own distinctive colour. First the red panel elapsed time, forty-four-thousand eight hundred and ninety-five earth days; distance to destination, eight-hundred and fifty-three—more than two years?

Why had I been awakened?

The Sansung particle drive seemed to be functioning perfectly, no evidence of emergency fuel rods having been brought into use. All long-range anti-meteorite screens were at full strength. I looked at the power consumption meters; these showed normal so I glanced at the units used. There was a discrepancy here from the estimated usage. I soon realised this could be accounted for by my own unscheduled defrost and the air-conditioning and lighting that would be operational throughout the great vessel. No cause for alarm; fuel was no problem.

The next panel was cargo; not the dead cargo of building materials, engineering tools, seeds and fertiliser and the host of other things that could be reasonably expected requirements to establish a new colony. But the live cargo. The live cargo consisted of hundreds of transportation modules similar to my own, three hundred and ninety seven to be exact. Each module was connected to the panel to the right of the main power indicators. Thermocouples showed that they were all within the allowable + or - 1% of -59c. This frigid temperature was cold enough to prevent all cell growth or ageing, but would still allow minute electrical currents to circulate the brain and with amplification to register on the panel. I was about to continue the routine when I became aware of Anthea close by; I never understood how Anthea made her presence known—I certainly had not heard her approach. On smooth surfaces such as the ship's deck her walk was completely silent. I recalled the first time I had seen Anthea; how seemingly effortless were her movements as she had danced. I quickly shut the memory from my mind. I could not afford to think of Anthea in the role she had then assumed, a sultry sexually stimulating creature of entertainment. Now, in her current capacity of scientific advisor, she drew my attention to the long-range scanner. This was forecasting a conjunction of trajectories; in plain English, a collision, in ninety-five hours. How could such an event come about?

Han Venturer was designed to change course to avoid objects in its path and must have taken evasive action hundreds of times in order to sweep round or over or under anything that its deflector screens couldn't despatch. Anthea seemed to read my mind: "I had the main computer check this analysis before I wakened you, Ro. It didn't take long—there was no need to search for data; and then it was simple calculus once I plugged to the long range scanners."

Simple I thought; considering the complexities involved. Well thankfully we were equipped with the finest example of earthly inventive genius since mankind's long climb from the ooze. I felt no need to question this statement.

CHAPTER TWO

───◆───

The 22nd century on earth opened to fanfares and celebrations. This was to be the century when mankind finally dominated the living conditions on this planet.

The D.R.A.K. had been invented!

Future weather patterns could not be controlled but at least could be accurately forecast, energy was plentiful and food was cheap.

Such was the popular myth. But another side to conditions existed; business operations had progressed into a few world-wide multinational conglomerates. The heads of these organisations were both highly motivated and ruthless.

Side by side with the legal confederations, multinational crime syndicates evolved; these, big business came to accept as being more profitable to endure than to fight.

This was the situation on earth when, towards the middle of the century one beautiful morning in May, not far from Lhasa the capital of Tibet, a small group of men paused to look around. The sunshine sparkled on the snow-capped mountains; the melt water gurgled in the streamlets before joining the wider rivers. But the scenery was of little consequence to Dr Serifimo Olletti who, along with two associates, was heading for the Sino Research Centre. He only paused to reassure himself on the remoteness of this area. He came to the centre to finalise a contract for new chemical filtration equipment which had been the subject of lengthy negotiations with the Italian company of which Dr Olletti was now head.

Serifi Olletti was a typical exemplification of the new age criminal. His father had taken great pains to instruct his son in the niceties of getting things done, his way, today!

Serifimo had been to the best schools, followed by the most expensive colleges, and along the way he learned how to manipulate his fellows. He had a natural talent in mathematics and in most of the scientific subjects he applied his mind to so he matriculated while still young. Then his father showed him how to run the "business."

With the death of his parent he found himself in control of a substantial organisation, but he was determined to better his Father, to make his own mark.

His hard face and even harder eyes glanced indifferently at the surroundings; today was to be the climax of his ambitions, and he was looking forward to his coming meeting. He had sufficient knowledge of chemistry to negotiate his way to the head of department at the institute, a Professor Lintoff.

The Sino Research Centre was as famous for its contributions to science as it was reticent about another unusual sideline, which it had founded. The Lhasa Pleasure Grounds. In order to understand this phrase it is necessary to go back many years. Tibet is a remote land, mountainous, bleak, isolated and with a small population. The climate, the terrain and the religious order of Buddhism have all played a part in keeping Tibet a backwater and something of an anachronism in the world. Many of the male population went into monastic orders leaving women with a more influential role to play in their country. Tibetans or High Bods, as they call themselves, are firm believers in reincarnation; the Dalai Lama, their spiritual head and leader, can trace his predecessors back for hundreds of years. So can the Po Mo, the only female to inherit a religious function.

Early in the twenty-first century the reigning Po Mo broke with tradition and sent her daughter to be educated in England. This remarkable female became the first of an outstanding line of chemical engineers.

These capable chemists developed an ingenious and simple device that automatically separated gold particles from the sediment in the river beds, and with the proceeds of this invention they established a research facility not far from Lhasa.

Notwithstanding the original chemical nature of the studies carried out here, this centre eventually became predominantly concerned with genetic research and development. The work of the institute was based on sincere motives, the investigation of cancer. This is where the Tibetans' unique isolation proved advantageous with ethical questions conveniently taking second place. Little communication with the outside world and a shortage of people made research into human beings a natural subject to explore. The divinity of the head of research meant there were no difficult moral questions to answer. Even the raw material was to hand; there has always been a slave trade in the poor areas of both China and Northern India—the only real difference being the extreme youth of the female children now required. On arrival at the institute's reception office the transaction was completed and payment was always made in gold.

A clinically austere doctor in an unusually frank interview once disclosed, we carefully measured and tested all human functions and this work eventually led us to become involved in embryo research. Again there did not appear to be any difficulties in obtaining embryos. The result of all this experimenting is well known—the famous Cancer Screen. It is commonplace today, but that was the original product that made the Sino Research Centre renowned throughout the world. The success of the cancer cure provided ample funding to allow for expansion of the centre's work to include the original chemical interests, in addition to the continued exploration of growth patterns and nucleoprotein research.

There was a fascinating by-product of the genetic experiments. The results of years of investigation added additional females to the population of the institute; females provided excellent experimental subjects because of earlier maturation than males. They were well fed and housed and this contrast to outside conditions encouraged a placid and willing acceptance of their state. They provided domestic labour and served other useful functions; for example, fulfilling the requirements of the pleasure grounds.

The party of Italians were in Professor Lintoff's office. "Well, can we get down to a final delivered price then?" asked the Professor. He was in no way inclined to haggle; there was no need, for money was no real problem and he didn't like Dr Olletti—there was something sinister about him. So the professor intended to conclude the business as quickly as possible. They were leaning over the table on which lay blueprints of the plant they were discussing.

"The price to include the initial training of our people so that we can install the equipment ourselves," went on Professor Lintoff.

"Certainly," Dr Olletti replied with a thin smile.

"However, there is one necessary preliminary before we can continue." He quickly looked at his two companions and noted that they stood immediately in front of the office door; no one could enter while they were in that position. The threat in his voice was unmistakable. The professor looked up in alarm but. he had no time to think or even move before Dr Olletti pulled the trigger on a small pistol he held in his hand. There was a muffled crack and the professor clasped his belly with both hands, his face contorted with pain. "What have you done?" he gasped, as he slowly sank to his seat.

"I have just signed our contract," Dr Olletti stated in a flat, harsh voice. "I'll give you a few minutes to get your breath back and then you will take me to see your leader."

The professor repeated, "What have you done?"

"I have implanted a small bomb into you." He spoke slowly and distinctly. "It is small but quite capable of blowing your guts into the face of anyone who tries to remove it. If any metal comes within 50mm it will detonate." He ignored the professor's painful attempt to stand. "Now, we wish to meet this leader of yours, the female with funny name."

"You mean the Po Mo?" moaned the professor.

"Yes," snapped Dr Olletti.

"I'll not do that, and even if I could, she never receives visitors."

"I think I have something here that will interest her," smiled Dr Olletti. He nodded to the largest of his companions who stepped forward to remove from his briefcase a slab of gold!

It was 300mm Square, and 30mm thick.

The professor gasped with surprise; even though gold was collected relatively easily from local rivers, a block as large as this exceeded anything he could possibly imagine. "So, you will send this little item to your Po Mo," sneered Olletti, "and say that we wish to speak with her."

"I'll do no such thing," declared the professor. "You can't buy your way into here."

"So, you need a little help," smiled Dr Olletti, his eyes closing slightly in anticipation. He pressed the button on a small case he kept in his coat pocket. The professor screamed in agony as a searing, nauseating spasm of sheer torture filled his body. He fell to the floor rolling and moaning in pitiful distress. He had thought of some beating or other show of force to make him comply with the wishes of this pitiless trio, but he could never imagine such pain as this. He fell to the floor, vomiting under the desk that he had rolled against; he lay curled in the foetal position, still groaning, but softly now.

The three standing all appeared to be enjoying the spectacle; their eyes sparkling, their heads thrust forward with mouths slightly open, they drew in long deep breaths.

After a while Dr Olletti nodded to the big man who stepped forward and brutally kicked the professor. "Get up," he snarled. The professor rose slowly to his feet. "How do you communicate with this Po Mo of yours?"

The professor nodded weakly towards the desk. "If anything urgent comes up I can use that."

"Something urgent has come up," sneered Dr Olletti, "and to make sure she realises, say that you are sending a specimen for her to see."

Professor Lintoff had neither the will nor strength to argue; he pressed the button of the communicator and spoke as he had been bidden.

"That's better," said the doctor. "Now call that pretty secretary we saw outside."

The Professor again did as instructed.

When the girl entered the office Dr Olletti said, "Please show my friend to the Po Mo. He will carry this for you." He nodded to the block of gold on the desk. "I don't expect you wish to carry it?"

The girl looked at the huge block in amazement and then at the professor for permission.

The professor stammered, "That's all right, Ching Ching, the Po Mo is expecting you."

Ching Ching sensed the unnatural atmosphere, but could think of nothing to say and so left the office. The big man followed with the gold. No one spoke for some ten minutes; then Ching Ching, who bowed and stood aside to allow a tall, august figure to make an entrance, opened the office door.

The Po Mo made an impressive sight. Her presence in the office changed the whole atmosphere; her dark hair was piled high on her head and was topped with a mantilla-like head-dress. She wore a dark-red pure silk robe that reached down to the floor, shimmering as she moved. She said nothing, glancing an enquiry towards Professor Lintoff. The professor, conscience stricken for his part in luring his leader to her doom, laid his head on his arms in shame. The Po Mo turned to face Dr Olletti. As she did so she received a pain bomb in her soft middle stomach; her eyes opened wide and with a small cry she collapsed to the floor. Her companion, a beautiful woman who constantly accompanied the Po Mo and whose function Dr Olletti quickly understood, was the next to receive the horrific shot. She screamed, and also collapsed to the floor. As the three Italians looked down at the women on the floor the door burst open and Ching Ching rushed in, only to stop in open-mouthed amazement at the scene she witnessed. With a muttered oath the big man strode rapidly behind her and chopped his hand savagely to the side of her neck. There was a sickening crack as Ching Ching's neck broke like a snapped twig.

"You fool!" snapped Dr Olletti.

The big man looked abashed. "She startled me," he muttered.

Neither man appeared concerned that a pretty young girl's life had just ended. Dr Olletti watched with narrowed eyes as his two companions completed the task of moving the Po Mo and her companion into two upholstered chairs. They were used to this sort of situation and quickly revived the two women with a short burst under the nose of each with an aerosol they carried.

"Now keep a good watch on the door this time," snapped Olletti. He addressed the Po Mo: "My organisation has decided to join forces with yours. There will be no apparent change of direction to the institute's work, but from time to time we may wish you to introduce an additional enquiry on our behalf. We wish to avoid attention, so your isolated position here is highly suitable for our business. I understand that you conduct all your administration by intercom and are rarely seen. That is perfect; take a good look at your new partner—I intend to live with you from now on!" Dr Olletti stood there waiting for the reaction that was sure to come.

The Po Mo, her voice unnaturally hesitant, stammered, "You cannot possibly be serious. You can't expect to get away with this?" Yet there was a questing in her statement. She looked across at Professor Lintoff. "Call the guards!" she snapped, something of her accustomed authority returning.

"I see that a demonstration is required," Dr Olletti spoke quietly, but with unmistakable menace in his tone. He directed his control at Pol Moa, the Po Mo's consort. Pol Moa shrieked in agony, her slender form arching backwards in the chair; then, her hands holding her midriff, she started to sob pitifully while tears coursed down her face making a hideous mess of her carefully made up features. The Po Mo jumped out of her chair to bend over her companion in an effort to comfort her.

Dr Olletti spoke again. "There are three levels of intensity to this little device; you have only experienced the lowest level. If you do not respond to my requirements immediately I will demonstrate the next stage. If ever I reach stage three, you may reasonably expect to die—after a suitable interval, of course." He paused. "We will continue to operate through your friend I think." Dr Olletti almost purred the words. "Yes, I'm sure she will serve our purpose admirably." He had never felt so contented in his life. Now he could revenge himself on a woman of substance, now he would make up for the humiliations of his earlier years when paid harlots only accepted him.

The Po Mo, all composure gone, held Pol Moa's head to her breast crying bitterly. From his seat behind his desk Professor Lintoff held his head in his hands. He slowly stood up and looked at these pitiless faces, the faces of the world's most ruthless criminals. He moved from behind his desk. Dr Olletti casually edged behind the other desk in the office. Professor Lintoff hesitated for a second, then blind fury contorting his face, he rushed at the big man.

The big man smiled. He waited calmly, his arms swinging loose, but instead of trying to strike his opponent the professor ducked beneath his arms and threw himself at the big man's body. He was quickly inside the man's guard; he had seen the gun partially concealed in his waistband.

He clung desperately to his neck, his hands clasped together, his legs wrapped around the big man's legs. Suddenly understanding, fear came into the big man's eyes as he realised the danger he was in. Too late! Even as he tried to throw the professor off, the metal of the gun triggered the explosive in the professor's body.

As forecast, the explosion was sufficient to blow a large hole in the professor's body, but in doing so, it did the same to the big man.

That made three fatalities within the hour, and that was the end. There was no more resistance.

Dr Olletti moved into the Po Mo's apartments, never to be seen again. This coup represented the climax of his ambition. He would now have everything any person could possibly require.

There is a militant type of mind to which the hostilities involved in any human situation seems to be its most interesting or valuable aspect, some individuals live by hatred as a kind of creed. Dr Olletti now had more influence in the world than any other individual. And he was opposed to anything that might change these conditions in any way.

He controlled a substantial proportion of the entire wealth of this planet, and he knew better than anyone that any imaginative adventures such as Space Exploration, which was being whispered about in certain academic circles, would make massive inroads on world-wide financial resources. Dr Olletti had no intention of allowing any activity which could adversely affect his personal wishes to develop anywhere on earth.

CHAPTER THREE

I allowed my mind to backtrack many years.

The D.R.A.K. was undoubtedly competent to deal with space navigation. It had been developed in the Sino research centre, where the discovery of the possibilities inherent in Zosite crystals led to multi-path-inter-formatting.

In short, The DRAK—or the ability to process several functions at once, just as the human brain to varying degrees has been doing for aeons. This amazing progression from the simple computer had come to dominate life on Earth.

I remembered our science teacher explaining to the class of young students about the unlimited calculating power offered. It seemed that there was nothing which The DRAK could not compute. An interesting study had noted that royalties from this invention would be greater than all the wealth of the rest of the world put together. This report was quickly stifled but was the beginning of the "Great Conflict."

A determined but mysteriously anonymous campaign emerged, with the undeclared resolve to restrict any further major scientific developments. The study disappeared and any newspaper or video station, which commented on the report suddenly, went out of business or changed owners. This was not immediately noticed by most people, who happily continued to speculate on the outcome of the most recent of the heroine's dilemmas in the current top soap opera; but there were alert minds who remembered what had happened. They noted that respectable publishers changed ownership at astronomical prices; someone had unlimited funds available to buy whatever they required at any price!

I thought about the background to the "Great Conflict". Was not THE DRAK the greatest advance science had ever made? Was it not available to all? The royalty of 1% on any development directly attributable to or directed by a DRAK was not unreasonable to further the work of Sino research.

Nationalism faded away as each major power bloc concentrated on creating riches for themselves. There was little need to steal from one's neighbour when with little effort and the help of DRAK fortunes were there for the taking. Interest rates had settled at 0.5 of 1% and had stayed there; solving inflation and casually eliminating one of government's greatest perks.

National governments became one more irrelevance; all major decisions were made between big businesses and big criminals.

Food shortages disappeared as DRAK produced accurate weather forecasts, as well as showing the areas where crops were best suited to develop and grow. Unlimited statistical information helped to genetically engineer new strains that resisted pests and diseases and produced abundant yields.

But the ultimate benefit was power.

All by the apparently simple conversion of hydrogen into its basic components. Most people on earth could have all that they could possibly wish for; of course, a mere 1% of these benefits went to Sino research.

The first indication of changes to come was World Wide

Investments. This organisation was formed when the sheer volume of money due to Sino research became more than the Director and the small board of management could handle.

No well-known figure ever appeared to head Sino research, for the organisation always shunned publicity. A company spokeswoman always made any announcements and blankly refused all attempts by the media to personalise the work. However, to the curious people who looked beneath the surface of world affairs, it was obvious that there was a sinister underground force at work. A force capable of changing the nature of stated government policies and which compelled the resignation of outspoken personalities who dared to enquire publicly, who was behind the bland façade that Sino research presented to the outside. Someone was very satisfied with conditions on earth as they existed.

I thought of the anomaly that the very words, Space Research, had been dropped from the language for many years; this happened even while eager young minds bursting with enthusiasm to learn more of the wonders of the universe could get no support from any authority.

In this same period, the mystery surrounding the disappearance of Bruce Star aroused speculation worldwide. Handsome, telegenic and popular, the news reporter foolishly announced that he had proof that organised crime was sheltering behind the edifice of Sino research! Shortly after this astonishing statement and before any details were added, a minor paragraph appeared in the world press stating that Bruce Star, in company with a small party of fellow skiers, had failed to return to their hotel one evening. The only theory regarding their disappearance was that they must have struck a treacherous crevasse area. But all ten? And all of them experienced skiers? A heavy fall of snow the same night blanketed all traces and no alarm was raised until the following day. Despite rumours, nothing more was heard of Bruce Star who joined the many other unwritten chapters in the story of Sino research.

Of course scientific conferences continued without the most fascinating topic of cosmology getting more than oblique references.

At one of the few international gatherings he attended, Ched Taylor's attention was attracted by an unusual presentation. He listened intently to Teng Ho Pot who gave an amusing talk on how he had discovered a method of converting Silver into Gold.

Ched was full of admiration for this new acquaintance, the physicist cum-alchemist. At table for their meal that evening, after a few preliminary observations, Ched enquired, "What are you doing at present?"

"Looking for an interesting pastime," laughed the other.

"I was hoping that you might have something to offer," Ched continued.

They found much in common to discuss, including their similar views on many of the world's current unsolved mysteries. Once the initial pleasantries were over they soberly remembered the facts of life. They went out to walk through the spacious grounds of their hotel. After a brief glance over his shoulder confirmed Ched's supposition that no-one was within hearing distance, he continued, "I get bitterly frustrated by all this nonsense about not being able to discuss space research." Teng Ho nodded, but muttered cautiously, "Don't forget that business of the chemist Jabo Fermanty. I don't know what you think but I will never believe that story about a little known malady that has remained unheard of until last spring!"

Just like Bruce Star, many a well-known figure had simply disappeared when they had seriously raised the question of exploring space. If they flew their own aircraft, it was likely to crash inexplicably. The mountaineers suffered equipment failure. Although these events never made headlines, the circumstances were sufficiently unusual to be noted in many educated circles and to achieve a stultifying effect. The two new friends continued their conversation into the night without either managing to add to their common knowledge.

Before returning to California, Ched invited Teng Ho to join a small camping party which would be held on an island off the Australian coast.

★   ★   ★

The restrictions on frontier scientific knowledge constituted the subject which arose and was thoroughly discussed during the course of this holiday on one of the lesser known islands of the barrier reef. A party consisting of myself, Roland Stern, Ched Taylor and Teng Ho, our respective wives and a recently acquired friend of the girls, a well-proportioned fair-haired and blue-eyed Teutonic female named Oval Himnal, formed the nucleus of the forthcoming conspiracy. This group set itself the target of shattering the restrictions which were so oppressive to the technical and enquiring mind. Three more couples arrived a few days later in their own yacht which remained peacefully at anchor in the beautiful blue waters of the bay. The bay was surrounded by a fringe of white sand, which brightened the otherwise dusty looking scrub stretching inland from the shore line.

Long lazy days always started with swimming and snorkelling, the hunters of our party quickly spearing sufficient fish to supply our needs. There would follow a barbecue on the beach cooked over a fire of driftwood and scrub brush.

The men boisterously competed to light a fire. Oval suggested she could do better and did. We men stung with embarrassment jumped on Oval and held her down. We then discovered her secret which consisted of a second silvered mirror with a hole through the centre. This arrangement as Oval demonstrated later could even melt sand if held steady for a little while. This was an early demonstration of Oval's abilities. After the fun and excitement of holding down Oval's athletic, six foot body had settled down, the day's main topic of conversation began: Space Exploration!

There were several days of generalities before our party decided to split into four groups, each of which had the task of solving a specifically identified basic problem concerned with the venture. The first hurdle was finance; most people had sufficient money to allow them to live as they wished, but for this scheme hundreds of millions of credits would be required: How could this sort of finance be raised?

Next was the question of personnel. The Project, as we had decided to call the result of our deliberations, would require the efforts of hundreds of hands and brains.

Who would be included?

Then thirdly, rockets being well understood to be out-dated, by what method or means could such a scheme be achieved?

And finally and by no means least, where could an enterprise such as we were contemplating be undertaken—and in view of the well-known antipathy that would be attached to such an enterprise—in secret?

CHAPTER FOUR

The financial difficulty was easily solved.

A by-product of my maritime experience involving the rescue of an underwater passenger liner that had become trapped while on a sightseeing voyage to the sub-Antarctic volcanoes constituted the "Green diamonds!" I gave my friends this unofficial version of the rescue operation.

"I couldn't ask for volunteers," I said, "so decided to go myself. I just refused to sail away and leave them stuck. It wasn't too difficult to get a line attached but when it came to swimming back to my own vessel fighting against the current, which had dragged the cruise ship into the mud, was another matter. However, by dragging myself along the tow-line I finally managed. On the way back I saw some peculiar looking round lava-like rocks. After we had rocked the passenger liner loose I went back for those boulders. They lay temporarily forgotten for weeks, in the hold of the ship.

"When the sensation of the rescue had subsided and during the writing of my official report on the incident, while striving to remember every detail, (there had been some talk of disciplinary action for endangering my craft), I recollected the rocks.

"During my next leave period, I took those rocks back home where I have a small laboratory which allows me to play about whenever I'm in the mood. I cut through the outer crust, then to my amazement I found a cluster of diamonds! There were lots of them!"

Diamonds were one of the few items on earth that still attracted real envy. It was no longer possible to employ a large labour force to dig out tons of rock to obtain a few carats of diamond. Most men found more congenial occupations, so the stock of diamonds increased very slowly. Because so many people had money to spend, demand grew out of all proportion to supply.

As I told my companions of this fortunate discovery, I added, "I have concealed all knowledge of this find until now; Beth is the only other person aware of the story."

With the announcement of this information, I casually tossed a couple of pea-sized stones onto the table. These stones were still in their natural unpolished state; however, the people around the table knew exactly at what they were looking. A gasp of astonishment went around the group. Lin Ho grabbed one and Oval the other. Lin Ho immediately started scheming about how she might get one of these for her personal use! All eyes opened with amazement as we stared at the gigantic gems. When the whole party had had an opportunity to examine the stones and the excited comments over the size and the green cast of these magnificent jewels had subsided somewhat, Ched finally put into words what we were all thinking. "Diamonds like this must be worth millions and millions."

"I expect so," I replied. "The reason I kept quiet was because I didn't need the money and had no intention of being involved in any more fuss and publicity. The media coverage of the liner rescue and the controversy about whether or not I had endangered the lives of my passengers was more than enough for me."

My face flushed and filled with anger as I recalled how different my actions were made to sound when quoted by a brilliant and unsympathetic counsel at the official enquiry. Beth, who was sitting next to me, found and squeezed my hand; she was aware of the bitterness I had suffered.

Teng Ho then spoke in his gentle and precise English. "I am sure that I can arrange for suitable facilities which would allow the furtherance of our project." All went quiet as Teng Ho continued. "During the course of a family celebration, several of my brothers by marriage were seriously discussing the possibility of space exploration. Toward the end of our debate, my distinguished parent-in-law who had listened without comment, interrupted to say that if ever his sons ventured beyond the talking stage he would support the scheme!"

The backing of the first minister of a country the size and power of China was a guarantee that anything was possible.

This was not altruism on Ho Chek's part. For many years he had been seeking an opportunity to make his presence felt on the world stage. He ate of the finest foods. He found no satisfaction in drinking himself stupid and no pleasure in participating in drug orgies. He dressed his wife and the extracurricular females of his household in the most expensive clothes; what else could the most powerful person on Earth wish for? He finally decided that he wanted, above all, to establish his name with something that would be remembered.

If space travel was frowned upon by the world at large, what could be better than to break the pattern? If such a project were successful, China and her leader would be certain of a place in history.

Ched was the next speaker. His group knew what to expect, but the rest of the party listened intently as he gave a resume of the progress made by a talented group who were following a line of enquiry into meta-physics at the Institute in California of which he was head. This group were experimenting with a phenomenon associated with ultra-high speed gyroscopes. This was the result of Ben Hoyt who directed the group, reading in an old copy of the *Britannica* of original research conducted by Einstein and deHaas. This was way back in 1905 and referred to an aspect of magnetism, which they called the giro magnetic ratio.

Put into simple terms, they sought evidence to support a proposition of a sensational nature.

With this theory to serve as a reference point, Ben's team continued to extend and develop it, and eventually came to speculate that when the circumference velocity of a gyroscope approached the speed of light the kinetic energy theoretically could change the polarity of the nuclei of the atoms of which the gyroscope was made, which in this case was iron. Remember that the earth with its iron core normally carries a negative charge owing to it orbiting its star the Sun. If a self-contained negative force field could be produced, the two like forces would oppose each other. As long as this force field has a lesser mass than earth, anti-gravity could be created. For several years the work had been theoretical; then one day, some months previously, Ben Hoyt and Si Lucas had excitedly called Ched's office and virtually demanded that he come immediately to see for himself the result of their efforts. Ched said, "I could tell by the elation in their voices, that something extraordinary was taking place. I hurried to the building where large voltages were frequently handled; for this reason the lab was well away from others to minimise the effects of the occasional mistakes that are known to happen. I was surprised at the silence. There were eight people in the room; not one of them spoke a word and all were looking at a circular object that appeared to be stuck to the ceiling. I had no sooner arrived than the faint hum, which was the only sound, faltered, and became an ear-piercing screech; the disc started to wobble, then a deafening explosion knocked everyone in the room to the floor. A large hole appeared in the roof and through the dust and floating bits of paper we could see the blue California sky!

At the inquiry which followed, Ben, with an innocent expression on his face, said, "We think that the bearing failed." He said nothing about the fantastic speed they had attained and that the gyro had probably vaporised!

When I left, Ched concluded to his thoughtful audience, saying, "They have their new lab and are feverishly trying to rebuild their demonstration model. If they succeed, anti-gravity will solve the space exploration problem forever! The major problem has always been to overcome inertia and get a vessel out of the earth's gravitational field."

The final question to be answered and one which caused more heated argument than progress, was how to select personnel? After days of debate and deliberation, the party agreed on the following principles.

There would be no passengers. All personnel must be capable of contributing to the enterprise. If the project were to succeed, that is, if space flight became possible, because of political considerations on earth it would be a one-way journey. This meant leaving Earth behind forever. So this was to be a colonising venture!

Beth Stern who was a psychologist by training and a humourist by nature, summarised the personnel profile.

"We are looking for hundreds of people," she stated, "who are young and fit, mentally and physically mature enough to have formed a stable relationship, but as yet without children or other responsibilities and having no emotional attachments to prevent them from leaving behind forever all that we know on earth. We need people who have achieved a high standard of education and are adequately trained in a skill, which a new colony will require.

"And to cap it all," she concluded, "we need people who can keep a secret."

CHAPTER FIVE

In the 21st century China had ditched all pretence of democracy and reverted to the method of government which had served the vast country successfully from time immemorial—the family dynasty.

If the male heir apparent demonstrated the slightest mental or physical signs of weakness of falling away from the cardinal purpose of ruling with ruthless determination, his own relatives would eliminate him. On one notable occasion the matriarch of the family, a particularly corpulent Chinese female, smothered her own son while still in his teens by rolling her massive pot-belly across his face because he was deemed to be too soft.

What a seventeen-year old was doing in his mother's bed is not officially known.

The present ruler of China, Ho Chek, was in no danger; he had run the country with steely mastery for twenty-five years—ever since the day that he had ensured his succession by "accidentally" allowing his elder brother to drown whilst they were taking part in an adventure vacation on the headwaters of the Yellow river.

China claims to be the first country on Earth to demonstrate a continuous line of progressive humanity. The line can be traced back for over four thousand years, with stone tools and fire as the earliest evidence of a natural ingenuity that is characteristic of the race. Over the centuries there have been many examples of this scientific curiosity which still persists and makes the present generation worthy successors to Peking Man.

The first of these achievements was the moulding of the world's earliest plastic material into cooking pots and other types of vessels. This they continued to develop until the very name China came to represent the ultimate in this art form.

Then paper was produced and this soon became an essential tool whereby the leaders of this vast area were able to maintain control of their people.

After paper came gunpowder, the original explosive used to celebrate state and family functions for decades, which had a history in China long before the rest of the world understood its potential.

Acupuncture was an ancient healing art, which had been practised for centuries, and was certainly the forerunner of our present-day psycho-anaesthesia.

With such an impressive background and with the benefit of positive direction, it was not surprising to find scientific China amongst world leaders at the end of the Twenty-First century—the century that completely changed planetary conditions and living standards.

Of course, China took as much credit for the benefits derived from the brainchild of the Sino research centre as it possibly could.   But the truth of the matter was that the centre was Tibetan founded and based; and Tibet placed great emphasis in maintaining its ethnic difference from China.

When Teng Ho introduced me together with Ched Taylor to discuss our plans with the Chinese head of state, we came in for acute scrutiny and questioning

Teng Ho had arranged this meeting with his implacable father-in-law Ho Chek, the president of all China.

This meeting, held in the utmost secrecy, was a notable success; it was a discussion by four men who were determined to get things done, not just talked about.

Our host immediately accepted the basic principle of space travel. A careful study of the green diamonds led to Ho Chek's enthusiastic agreement to market these remarkable gems; he was in a perfect position and possessed the necessary acumen to feed them carefully into the world system. He knew how to build up a rarity demand and take his percentage along the way. He asked if there were any more to be obtained and I explained that no other person was aware of the existence or location of my discovery.

He stated categorically, "With the sole marketing rights, finance would present no difficulties; you can have whatever you want!"

The third item on the agenda was finding a suitable site: Teng Ho suggested a remote place in an area situated in Sin Kiang province, a desert region north of the Charmen Tagh mountains. The nearest named settlement was a collection of mud huts known as Makha. Ho Chek nodded his agreement. The Chinese leader would also arrange for military protection since Sin Kiang province was adjacent to Tibet and China's northern border so China maintained a strong military presence in the area at all times.

Thus in a very short space of time, arrangements were concluded for the start of man's greatest exploit. It had been so simple: we could hardly believe the list of achievements we would be able to report back to the rest of our party.

This second meeting took place almost twelve months

later on the same island in the Barrier reef where the original idea had been discussed. The light-hearted atmosphere however was no longer in evidence. Although solid progress had been achieved, now that action was required and not just casual holiday talk, some cautious soundings had taken place, and this gave cause for concern; there was an overpowering aura of impending danger.

This aura was most apparent when a review of progress on the work of the anti-grav project came up for discussion. Ched Taylor shared his apprehension with the rest of us. He explained that the development team led by Ben and Si were allocated a new lab in which to continue their work after the explosion of their experimental model. Although fresh buildings and facilities were readily available, the technicians were from a different section of the university to the original ones. Two of these technologists were quite bright; Ben wondered why the personnel department had included such high grade helpers and told me the following story:

"One evening when we had left the lab for the day, I remembered that I'd left my briefcase behind. I'm in the habit of reviewing the day's efforts during a relaxing sauna at home. Realising what I'd done, I returned to the lab. I slipped my identity card into the door control; the door opened quietly and I could see the senior technician photographing the blackboard which is still the standard means of illustrating theories and arguments. I'd spent the best part of the day in front of that board, scribbling and removing calculations then recalculating in the symbols we use for this specialist work.

"'What are you doing?' I demanded.

"Senior technician Lazerous spun round in confusion, his lank black hair hanging over his narrow forehead; he looked as guilty as sin.

"'I-I-I was just taking notes for my personal studies,' he quickly explained. 'I find this work so interesting that I wanted to record the calculations before you clear them off tomorrow.'

"Normally I would have thought no more about it. The explanation was quite in order, but there was a shifty look about this man. I knew instinctively that he was lying. However, there is no secrecy in what we're doing and so I let the matter drop—but something is not right!"

Ched Taylor had immediately realised the fantastic potential for their discovery but apart from the project group, had carefully kept his thoughts to himself. He said, "Ben is a scientist pure and simple; all he thinks about are his present problems, namely, how to design a gyroscope that will not fuse its bearings under the stresses that he is trying to impose.

"Nonetheless, that evening's affair forced me to consider other events, which I've tried to ignore.

"Why for instance has Professor Gunter shown so much interest recently in what we are doing? Of late Gunter had not only tried to engage Ben in conversation but had suggested transferring one of his own bright students to work with the specialist group. This offer Ben firmly refused; he had enough on his mind working with people who had been with him for years without taking time off to bring a newcomer up-to-date however bright he may be. The outlandish theories they were currently developing were an entirely new area of physics. Ben and Si have discussed with me a different atmosphere that hangs over the group's work but are unable to arrive at a conclusion; I'm very much aware of the situation. I was noncommittal when asked for an opinion, but I've taken steps to free the experimenters from as much outside interference as possible."

Now at the island conference, Ched made no bones about his real concern. "Somebody is making a determined effort to find out as much as possible about this whole anti-grav concept," he stated flatly. "I consider that the time has arrived when future progress will be dependent on a secure environment."

On this sombre note the first day's discussions came to an end; our party broke into small groups to go fishing, swimming, beachcombing or one of the other more usual holiday activities.

The following day our whole group concentrated on what proved to be the most difficult task to date, namely that of finding a formula to decide on the composition of the crew. For the past year members of the cabal had each been thinking long and hard about this question. What sort of people would we wish to start a new life with? It was difficult enough trying to select one partner, let alone an entire community. Facing up to this question made for a gloomy start to the proceedings.

Now that difficult decisions were required all present realised the need to formalise our business and Roland Stern was elected to chair the meeting. I was the eldest person present; I smiled to myself and wondered if my age was so obvious that this was the reason why I had been selected.

I didn't consider that my direct manner of speaking and forthright rejection of difficulties made me an obvious choice.

I started by saying, "I think that the starting point will be to decide on total requirements."

After some discussion a number of four hundred was generally accepted. We then went on to agree that any person who was prepared to leave this world behind to risk their lives on a completely unproved venture such as was envisaged, must have sufficient character to be a worthwhile companion or mad! "And I'm sure we can eliminate the mad ones," smiled Lin Ho Pot who together with Eva and Beth shared a great deal of experience in dealing with psychological situations. We then went on to consider in greater detail who was to be invited to join us.

Ched was confident that all the personnel involved with the work on the anti-grav experiment would be eager to see the consummation of their years of effort. Other members of the group put up similar suggestions; eventually it was agreed that each of the thirteen present would aim to recruit between ten and twenty people. Everyone realised how dangerous this activity would be; we all had first-hand knowledge of friends or colleagues who had simply disappeared after talking about taboo subjects! But for all the apprehension, we had no doubt whatever of gaining an enthusiastic response.

Throughout the educated world social gossip invariably returned to the restrictive and repressive force, which stifled so many aspects of inquiry. This project group had personal knowledge of many contemporaries who chafed under this blanket of suppression.

Ro Stern is in his middle thirties, of medium height and stockily built. A man of firm decisions and confident in his opinions once he has applied his mind to an idea.

I had sneered at myself when I had taken an extra year at Cambridge without finding a prospective future career any nearer to realisation. I entered a research centre more in hope of developing an interest than with any thought of remaining permanently; this was according to the exhaustively detailed report on me that had been made on Ho Chek's order:

The intellectual challenge offered with the advertisement for naval trainees was the sole reason for his entering such a traditional occupation, long contested by the sons of sons of naval families. His strong physical aura ensured that he is never overlooked in whatever company he finds himself. Females especially first glance and immediately looked again in fascination. This is a feature of his natural physical impact, which he takes for granted and rarely responds to. His prominent blue eyes are not the only unusual feature of this extraordinary man. If he were ever to think about it he would consider himself unaggressive, but his broad square jaw structure gives decidedly determined support to the statements he makes. He is conscious of this positive attitude once he is aroused to speak his mind. Therefore he tries to avoid giving pain to others whom he considers to be reluctant to face squarely unpalatable facts and their inevitable consequences. He gives the impression of being a surprisingly quick decision maker; this is his real strength but it causes many others to think of him as shallow. However, few people realised how much time and thought Roland Stern applies to most of the consequences, which he foresees as the obvious result of the question under discussion. It is difficult for other people to understand how another mind can analyse all relevant facts to reach a considered opinion as rapidly as Ro Stern does. He holds a passionate interest in justice and social responsibility, which stand in curious contrast to his marked lack of desire for close contact with his fellow men and women. He is vaguely aloof from both family and friends and could never ally himself with his country of birth or any political cause. He finds this detachment and isolation bitter at times, cut off from the sympathy and understanding of others, but is sufficiently compensated by his independence from the opinions and prejudices that appeared to dominate the world. A deep emotional need which he has never succeeded in qualifying to his own satisfaction lies always just beneath the surface of his thoughts.

(A detailed psychological and personal assessment indeed—how had it been obtained?) Now in the hot midday sun under a tall Eucalyptus, I let my mind roam back over my past life. I must review my commitment to this extraordinary affair—this project which I was instrumental in pursuing as eagerly as anyone. Was this really what I wanted from life? I must be absolutely sure of my own thoughts and wishes in order to be able to speak convincingly to others.

I considered my current prospects; how long would I remain satisfied driving an expensive holiday cruise ship? I was in no doubt that there was no future for me in this, never!

I already realised that I would soon become desperately bored with the inane chatter, which it was now my duty to participate in, pretending to find all that the tourists wished to speak about interesting and worthy of a polite reply. Surely the possibilities which were now being actively discussed however impractical they may seem at present must offer a richer prospect than anything else that I could possibly imagine!

After an unremarkable childhood and general schooling Beth Holman and I met at Cambridge, that famous forcing house of mental stimulation. A desultory relationship developed which ran into our final year. I realised that I was still looking for an objective in life and although I felt strongly attracted to Beth, by mutual consent, we separated each to follow individual paths.

Beth was expected to follow her Father's speciality in neurology. However, after twelve months of intensive study, she found that tracing nerves in dead frogs together with their associated chemical and electrical paths and interconnections far too exacting for her personal inclinations. She wanted to work with warm living people. Needing time to contemplate, she joined a mixed party of freethinking souls on a trek across Europe and then through the Middle East, only leaving the group when she reached India. Here she became interested in and found herself helping at a local orphanage, run by a long-established Catholic group. The orphanage was Catholic in every sense and as she became more deeply involved with the demanding but satisfying work, she often found it more convenient to spend the night at the convent. As there were neither facilities nor thought of accommodation for mixed couples, her long established bed partner took umbrage and left for greener pastures. Beth was upset for the first few days of separation but as with many females quickly found distraction at the nursery. She quickly overcame her sexual instincts and forgot everything in a headlong plunge into the problems of children deprived of natural parents. To introduce them into the harsh outside world with some degree of confidence was her objective. For however the nuns tried to give the children in their care a happy and satisfying upbringing, there was something missing. Something that good food and clothing and a love of God, could not replace. Beth threw herself heart and soul into this work, spending long hours in the library after the children were in bed to find what others had discovered before.

Some months later Mother Superior called Beth to her office.

"I've been wanting to discuss your future, my dear," she started, "you work too hard, you try to do too much, you need moral stimulation. I would like you to attend spiritual support classes with Father O'Neil."

The effect on Beth was like a cold shower!

She suddenly realised what she had been doing for the past year. She had been hiding. Hiding from her father and friends at home, trying to hide from herself. The thought of becoming a nun and living here for the rest of her life made her shiver with revulsion. It was as if a shutter had been lifted; suddenly everything became clear. She now accepted the fact that she had been putting off the showdown with her father, having to witness the pain she knew that he must suffer. He had made no secret that he expected Beth to follow the family tradition of three generations.

Now the words of Mother Superior forced her to face the truth; she must have been subconsciously thinking of the future, and she realised that the scene with her father was inevitable.

Beth quietly but firmly told the head of her decision to leave, made a tearful farewell from her fellow workers and sadly parted from the children who had come to mean so much to her. The following day she started for home.

On her way through London she met me.

Beth was astonished at the intense feeling of pleasure that ran through her as we greeted each other in the transportation concourse. She had never thought of Ro as being handsome, but now dressed in a navy blue uniform, full of confidence, my stride denoted power and self-assurance.

As Beth took in the details of the strong fair hair tufting rebelliously skywards above my forehead, piercing eyes and generous mouth, and coupled them to our long period of separation, she realised just how much she had been missing. Her heart seemed to miss a beat; her skin became covered in goose pimples.

These violent emotions surprised her so much that she found difficulty in speaking.

"It's the long journey and the strangeness of being back in England," she told herself.

"You look a bit woozy Beth, let's sit down." Following these words with action, I gently led her to the sitting area. When we were seated I continued talking, passing quickly through my recent activities. I explained that after leaving Cambridge I had gone into the laboratories of World G.E.C. I told her how with several months of wholehearted effort behind me and nothing to show for it, my interest in pure science began to wane and how I had surprised myself as much as my colleagues at the labs when I decided to investigate an advertisement for marine engineers.

"And I'm on my way now for a try out cruise before final assessment," I finished. "Now tell me about yourself."

Beth was grateful for the interlude; she had barely heard what I was saying. She was desperately trying to sort out her emotions. Now she was remembering the months, which had run into nearly two years when we spent all our leisure time together. She knew that she was blushing. She remembered how happy she'd been when we were together, the college dances, the student socials and of course the two camping holidays, one in Scotland, the other in France, when we had only each other for companionship. She was daydreaming happily when my question brought her back to reality. Slowly she went through her activities of the past eighteen months. When she came to the part where Mother Superior had tried to enrol her into a formal relationship with the church I smiled and looked up with interest. As she related the outcome I found her hand and gently squeezed it; for both it was an electrifying contact. As Beth continued to relate her coming confrontation with professor Holman, she suddenly stopped. "Ro," she gasped, "let's get married!"

She thought, "If Ro's attached to anyone else, I'll die!" There was no need to worry.

"I wondered how long you could resist me!" I laughed. "I think we've waited long enough."

Less than an hour later we parted, each to deal with our own immediate programmes, but we both had that inner glow of total commitment to another person. For Beth it was as though a heavy burden had been lifted from her shoulders. She realised the disappointment her father would feel at her decision. The prospects of her forthcoming marriage, however, caused all other matters to fall into proper perspective.

We were married in her local church six weeks later. We neither held any religious beliefs but the ancient building added a certain atmosphere to the civil formalities, which were the norm these days. We were content in the solemn ceremony and a feeling of fulfilment, which we both were determined to maintain. And thus began a perfect relationship which was to continue to the end of our lives.

So, now lying on the beach warmed by the hot sun, looking over the Coral Sea, our thoughts seemed to mingle; without speaking Beth knew that I was concerned about getting the timing of the ultimate decision right as well as the possible consequences once recruitment started.

I guessed that Beth was considering the design of a programme, which would help the selection team to pick out human weaknesses, which could develop into shattering explosions of guilt and anguish in the enforced loneliness that members of the expedition would face.

My hand reached out for Beth's

"Have we time before dinner?" I murmured.

CHAPTER SIX

To enable the project to commence, a temporary base was required; this would include premises in which to interview prospective ventures and an office from where orders for the masses of equipment that would be required could be organised. The Chinese president Ho Chek took this request for help in his stride; it took him no more than one week to find and subsequently to offer for our use suitable accommodation which would enable us to commence our adventure.

Provisional H.Q. would be on Hainan, an island off the coast of China. This was large enough to have port facilities for easy acceptance of the vast quantities of stores and materials that would be required for the project, but being an island, afforded some security. Strange faces and new arrivals were soon noticed. The island came within Mainland Chinese Military jurisdiction and Ho Chek arranged to increase this supervision to previously unheard of proportions. I was relieved by the security which this afforded, but at the same time concerned by the attention such a high military presence would attract; after some little thought I shrugged—I couldn't expect to have everything just as I wished.

The H.Q. was a 16th century castle with several outbuildings and a surrounding wall. It was a relatively simple matter to fence off the whole area and display notices to the effect that the property was closed for repair work to be carried out.

Once the organisation was established, I spent most of my time working with Lin Ho Chek, who dealt easily with the intricacies of Chinese officialdom. She had not lived all her early life in the shadow of her father, attended state banquets and official functions, flirted with young officers and civil servants, without finding out how to get things done.

I wondered what the background circumstances were. I never ceased to marvel at the manner in which stiff dignified mandarins, who had held me up for days demanding application forms and documents of all sorts, suddenly melted like ice-cream under hot lights when Lin Ho came onto the video phone to ask sweetly, "Will there be any difficulty?"

Lin Ho smiled as she cut the connection; she knew perfectly well that there would be no problem. She glanced up at me and smiled once more; she had no intention of explaining why she was so confident in getting her own way. She had already noted mentally that Ro Stern would need a different approach to her previous techniques, and the prospect of a challenge amused her.

Jiang Zemin would do far more than cut through a bit of red tape to keep on the right side of Lin Ho. She allowed her memory to drift idly back to the evening when she allowed Jiang Zemin to "take her".

The main event had occurred in a summerhouse on one of the many fragrant, multi-coloured islands in the ornamental lake of the imperial palace. She almost laughed out loud as she remembered the devastated look on Jiang's face when the gardener shone his lantern into the summerhouse to reveal the Chief of Staff bumping the president's daughter!

A source of amusement throughout the palace was the manner in which the chief of staff and protocol was watched and dominated by his wife:

Yen Zemin restricted his out-of-office-hours activities to strictly house and garden; he didn't even have a holiday wife. Then to be caught on the job, by one of the lowliest members of his staff: Lin Ho had arranged for and paid the gardener on three previous occasions to wait for this particular night.

The advice Lin Ho had received from her father's premier mistress had found fertile ground when she had said, "Always keep at least one ace up your sleeve when you play with men."

During Lin Ho's formative years of adolescence, she had played the man-game with ruthless enthusiasm; many of the top government officials had sons who would follow their parents into government administration, and what better start to their career than to marry into the family of the president?

However, they met more than their match when they tried to boost their position through an attachment to Ho Chek's daughter. She accepted all potential suitors with unrestrained gusto; she was genuinely willing for them to whisper their dreams and ambitions into her delicious ear as they lay atop this beautiful and priceless young woman. None succeeded however in gaining what they most desired, and when they eventually realised that this delicate butterfly which they wished so earnestly to net had lightly floated on to the next person in line they began to wonder if they had been less than prudent to have confided so passionately their private dreams and ambitions.

Lin Ho was a true daughter of her father and a natural

schemer; she kept careful notes about the secret ambitions, which tumbled from the panting lips of her wishful lovers. She quickly learned how to use these secrets to eliminate the social obstacles, which cropped up from time to time once she was given the task of organising official gatherings and banquets. The officious chief-of-police was easily persuaded to drop his insistent demand to be seated next to Ho Chek when Lin Ho slyly murmured, "I wonder if Ho Chek has heard that you have ambitions to succeed him at an early date?"

After a few years of manipulating her immediate entourage the pleasures began to pall and Lin Ho decided for herself that she wished to marry and set up a home to enable her to move onto the next stage in life, the broody phase. She started to cast around for a mate; but she would decide who it was to be! Anyone connected with politics was out; anyone without a substantial income would have been suspected of marrying her for her well-known wealth. This narrowed the field considerably; finally she met Teng Ho Pot.

Other than his proven talent as a scientist he had an unusual commercial ability for an intellectual, which allowed him to create a fortune for himself with judicious use of some of the ideas, which flowed from his inventive mind. He delayed making known that he had discovered a simple method of realigning the molecules of silver by increasing nucleic weight in order to form a new metal—a metal that was indistinguishable chemically from gold! He was sufficiently astute to ensure his own future wealth and after doing so passed on advance information to Ho Chek before making his method public.

In view of this early warning to a grateful Ho Chek and thereby gaining access to the palace circle, it is debatable if

Lin Ho was as truly discriminating as she had thought herself when she decided to take Teng Ho as her final and permanent partner. However, she now wore a contented smile as she remembered the events from her early life.

My wife Beth, together with Lin Ho and Eva Myelin who was married to Ched Taylor, spent many months compiling a screening programme for the D.R.A.K. junior, which they had acquired. The object of this programme was to alert the operators to potential weaknesses or even gaps in a candidate's personality. The weaknesses searched for were concerned with the ramifications on the individual psyche or soul when faced with the dramatic prospect of leaving behind forever all contact with their culture, history and previous associations. Naturally any computer programme is worth little or nothing until it has data to work with. To obtain all relevant information concerning a person's whole life involved hours of questioning. New recruits had their first taste of intensive interrogation once they arrived at the Hainan reception centre. Because of the fear of spies, the first questions were always: "What do you know of this project? Where did your information come from? How did you find this base?" Interviewees were seated in a comfortable chair and asked to place their hands onto indentations in the arms. Censors registered pulse rate, temperature and perspiration. They were told to look straight ahead into a mobile 3D picture, which concealed a camera; this focused onto the retina of the subject's eyes. This gave guaranteed identification; for many years retina registration had become compulsory at birth. The arrangements also provided additional information about a person's emotional condition. Genetic information was automatically gleaned from each subject's perspiration. Although there was no specific standard to meet, sufficient knowledge of many genetic variables was well-established and propensities could be forecast with a great deal of accuracy. Standard tables of attributes and weaknesses had been incorporated into the "Personnel Necessary Minimum Requirement" section of the computer selection programme. The P.N.M.R. had already rejected a number of candidates for the project, either on the grounds of suspected mental instability, or unconvincing background stories.

These rejects posed the leader and examiners with a serious dilemma. If they were told that they were not acceptable and allowed to go on their way, some details of what was planned were bound to leak; the very fact of them having been rejected guaranteed this. For a while these rejects were told nothing other than that further examination of their case was required to complete the interrogation and please to continue residing in the hotel which had been wholly taken over for the use of the new organisation. However they were bound to notice sooner or later that most of their fellow guests left suddenly without saying good-bye.

Ho Chek, leader of the world's largest community, settled this problem as he had so many others by the simple expedient of having the rejects classified as illegal immigrants! This was a serious offence throughout the world and severe measures were taken to deal with offenders. The practice in China was twelve months incarceration in a remote detention centre; followed by return to the country of birth—with no exceptions!

It was I, Ro Stern, who had to make the final decision to accept this way out of the dilemma we faced. I felt utterly wretched afterwards. It was completely contrary to my natural instincts, but I was learning fast that to get things done some principles had to be sacrificed. It also gave me an invaluable insight into government practices. "How many other inconveniences were held in captivity to satisfy the personal whim of a powerful political person?" I wondered.

Beth, Eva and Lin were also affected when they realised the fate to which an unsatisfactory result of the new volunteers would condemn their rejects to. This was the only explanation for their failure to apply the most rigorous reasoning to the story which the Bhuto's presented when they applied to join the project and who therefore, managed to slip through the screening process. Devlin Bhuto and his wife Nerfeti had both obtained degrees in Electrical Engineering from the "University of Calcutta". Devlin Bhuto had graduated with exceptionally high marks; he could easily have continued his studies to an honours level, but he was ambitious for worldly wealth and a taste of the good life. He was an avid reader of the magazines, which catered for dreamers and the envious and was anxious to join the comfortable style of living, which abounded all around them. He had an excellent start in life; born into the wealthy household of a senior civil servant, passing confidently through school and university, he and his wife Nerfeti made an extraordinarily handsome pair and they were accustomed to attracting attention wherever they went. The first position Devlin Bhuto was offered, that of teaching senior students who came from many differing castes and all levels of Indian society, he dismissed with a sneer—as "an affront to my superiority and knowledge." He immediately looked around for a more suitable post and was attracted by a video advertisement seeking recruits for a little-known company in Northern Italy. He smiled as he thought of how he had implied "that he would only consider the post if his wife was taken on as well." They were both accepted; the money was good and they soon developed an expensive style of living. They were looking at a luxurious villa on Capri when they were approached by a smooth-faced, smooth-talking, fancily dressed sallow featured young man who introduced himself as "Count Mattesi", adding, "Would you be interested in a little sideline which paid well together with bonuses for anything special?"

A monthly report on the progress being made at the labs attached to the factory at which they were employed was all that was required. Devlin Bhuto didn't know that his wife had been as thoroughly checked out as he had been before any approach was made.

"Okay," Said Devlin. His sense of guilt was soon forgotten when he calculated that now they could afford the villa.

This was how they were added to Dr Olletti's long list of industrial spies. Two years later the Bhuto's were told of the recruitment campaign for Project Pegasus. "We can promise you unbelievable wealth if you successfully sabotage the scheme," Count Mattesi murmured confidentially. Devlin Bhuto's greed knew no bounds; he eagerly accepted this golden opportunity. His new paymasters went to great lengths to train him for his deadly mission and to provide a watertight cover story. His target was the power plant; the techniques he practised would convert the generating unit into nothing much less than a Hydrogen bomb!

Devlin Bhuto was an apt pupil; both he and his instructors were confident in his abilities, but they all realised that gaining admission to the project was the principle hurdle. He was told, "There are others who you can contact for additional help if necessary once you're inside the organisation." He was impatient to start but his chief instructor made his position crystal clear. "We have a substantial investment in you, Dr Bhuto, and we will not risk this until we are convinced that events are in our favour."

Many months passed before conditions were considered suitable and he was adjudged ready to fire! When Bhuto and his wife eventually appeared at the Hainan reception centre, they followed several groups of rejects; this had left their interviewers in a melancholy mood and made them a degree less critical and thus more receptive of his carefully rehearsed background story. He easily passed the Personal Minimum Necessary Requirement section. He was not at all worried about leaving everything he had behind; he had no intention of leaving earth.

One of his fellow infiltrators, Walit Hussain and his wife, had preceded them by two days. Fortunately for the Bhuto's they heard nothing of the consequences of the Hussain's entry to Pegasus, until they themselves were safely inside making acquaintances with genuine New World Venturers.

CHAPTER SEVEN

The fateful decision had been made—the decision to attempt the construction of a space vessel; a vehicle capable of penetrating the furthest limits of the visible universe, the great unknown!

This was to be attempted not as an all-embracing effort by the entire population of earth, but by a minute fraction of those inhabitants and against the wishes of at least one of the world's most powerful organisations. Ro Stern, Ched Taylor and Teng Ho, all had first-hand experience of the forces against which the enterprise would be in direct conflict. However, the rest of the founding members knew little of the hazards that lay ahead.

This particular period was at the time when glowing reports appeared about the benefits, which were in store for the Canadian chemical industry. They were about to obtain access to the rich raw material of Alaska. The interest was due to the successful conclusion of the massive pipeline project, which had taken five years and much effort to complete.

News of this gigantic engineering project filled the media and was hyped up to stimulate excitement. All news these days was made to fulfil a role in the vast entertainment industry, which seemingly dominated life on earth. It was these reports, which led Ched Taylor to Canada. Here he succeeded in recruiting civil engineer MacGreggor, the first independent professional for the prospective enterprise. This appointment was for the key position of site engineer for the project; the first key position to be filled from a source outside the immediate circle of founders of the undertaking...

The principle was simple; it started with driving ten-metre lengths of sheet piling into the desert floor; excavation of a wide trench behind the piling followed, and then the self-propelled-winch would trundle to the centre and extend its brace arms to the full extent of the piling support. After this preparation all that was required was for a truck to tow the cable two kilometres from the winch to the point that the previous section had reached; this cable was connected to the free end of a drum of pipe; then a phone call through to the winch. "Okay Mike, start pulling." A plough device dug into the sand to a depth of one metre and the pipe followed. A pump fitted with a self-contained power source at the end of the pipe and it was possible to lay ten kilometres each day.

Forty-five days was not bad, thought MacGreggor—to get water from the Charmen Tahg Mountains to the site of his latest construction project. Mac was watching the last pump being covered with sand. "Tomorrow after the dry, dusty wind had been at work, there would be nothing to show where all this activity had taken place," he mused.

A field buggy tore towards them. Mac grinned to himself: there was only one person that drove like that in this heat and dust. Hank jumped out of the buggy. "They've started to inflate, Mac!" he shouted.

"Okay. We've finished here, let's take a look."

"I'm dying to see this thing up," yelled Hank.

Mac nodded. He was curious himself. It was this totally new concept that had been the deciding factor for him taking this job; he thought sourly that he had soon discovered plenty of reasons to cause him to wonder if he had made a wise decision.

Again, the idea was simple. Imagine a giant balloon cut in half and the flat half secured to a massive concrete base; then concrete would be sprayed over the balloon and allowed to set. Once the concrete had hardened, doors or any other openings that were required could be chopped through the shell and in a relatively short space of time one building would be ready for internal fitting out. The interesting feature about this balloon building was the size. It was 200 metres in diameter; that meant that it would be 100 metres high.

"And that," thought Mac, "is some balloon!"

"The critical part of this design is to ensure solid foundations," stressed the design engineer.

Mac simply said, "Give me the specification and I'll see that it's followed."

"Yes," nodded the designer, "that's why you were selected for the job."

This comment took Mac back to his previous project; which was the construction of a giant pipeline from Alaska across the frozen tundra and down to the chemical plants of Canada. He remembered the secretive approach that had been made to recruit him. This was because, they had told him, that this work was unusual and something special. It was special all right: this entire set up was the most peculiar organisation he had ever been employed by. Not for the first time he wondered if he had made a terrible mistake and furthermore he was responsible for bringing Hank with him:

Mac recalled the episodes, which led to Hank Hertzman becoming involved in the construction industry. At the age of eighteen he had dropped out of the education system shortly after his mother was killed in a holiday-weekend motor pile-up. Although he got along well enough with his father, the emotional shock came at what is a volatile period of a young man's life. The times when strange stirrings inside his head and body were particularly unsettling. He could not face the prospects of going through the local college and returning each evening to a house that was no longer a home. He decided to look for wider horizons.

Early one morning Hank took his hiking pack and leaving a brief note for his father promising to write, headed north. By listening to stories of truckers eager for an audience to share their lonely journey, Hank decided to make for the coalfields of Alaska. They sounded exciting and sufficiently far away from home and sad memories.

Some days later he was in a wayside diner, which offered cheap basic accommodation to hikers, wanderers and long-distance truckers. It was situated along the route of the great intercontinental highway that ran from Chile through Central America, Mexico, California, and on into Canada, thence to Alaska and finally ending at the outskirts of Anchorage.

Hank was out early next morning looking around the lorry park when he was attracted by the sound of hammering on iron. Following the sounds he found a tired looking man struggling to loosen the nuts on one of the double wheels of his giant trailer. Hank offered help; this was acknowledged with a bitter oath. With Hank pulling on the lever of the wheel wrench whilst the driver aimed savage blows at it with a sledgehammer, they managed eventually to remove the wheel nuts. "They put these things on in a nice warm garage with power tools and never worry about how we're supposed to get them off by hand and in freezing weather," grumbled the trucker. A further hour was needed to fit the spare wheel onto the massive trailer then return the damaged wheel to its carrier; these efforts left man and boy sweaty and dirty so they returned to the dormitory block to shower. Afterwards while ploughing through a gigantic breakfast of beefsteaks, bacon and four eggs, Hank told his story to his new acquaintance, the trucker called Dave.

Dave listened quietly, then told Hank:

"My usual mate developed violent stomach cramps two days ago and I had to take him to the nearest hospital. I decided to carry on by myself rather than wait for a replacement because they pay for a tight delivery schedule; then I had to get this blowout on a so-and-so wheel," he added bitterly. "It's a chance in a million to get a dud tyre; and on an inside wheel too! However I need a mate—the job's yours if you want it." Hank jumped at the opportunity—and so started his working life as a trucker's mate.

Dave's load consisted of long sections of pipe. These were a metre in diameter; the walls were so thick and the pipe so heavy that the largest trucks could only haul three sections to a full load. They were destined for an ambitious scheme to bring the abundant coal deposits of Alaska to the chemical plants of Canada, which were hungry for such rich raw material.

Then followed five weary days of monotonous driving. The scenery was spectacular, with bubbling crystal-clear streams rushing along rocky indentations worn into the mountain shoulders and in between clefts at the foot of the peaks to begin their long journey to the Pacific. The hillsides were a solid mass of dark green up to the snowline; here the remains of last season's snows still lay on the mountain's higher slopes. At road level the lime-stained milky-blue lakes were still and silent, watchful as mirrors, duplicating the mountain scenery. Dave had seen it before so often that the spectacle no longer affected him; he only wanted to get back home to his wife and family.

Hank, in between desultory observations by Dave, which reminded him of his father, thought about his mother; he pretended to sleep to hide the tears that stung his eyes.

They arrived at the base construction camp of "Transpipe," the consortium that were laying the pipe line around midday.

Dave went to report to the receiving office, and to register his load. He returned extremely unhappy; he was paid by delivery and timing, and the delay with the wheel had caused him to lose most of his bonus. He decided to remain in camp overnight and make an early start to his return journey the following morning. He had agreed to introduce Hank to the camp manager who went by the name of MacGreggor. Mac, as he was generally known, was far from receptive; he remembered thinking at the time about how he was running a skilled operation to a tight schedule and could see little use for a young man who knew nothing at all about the business. However, he did know Dave who had a daughter who had caught Mac's fancy, so a little later Hank was reluctantly set on as casual labourer and general dogsbody.

The main workshop was an important section of the base where major repairs and plant maintenance was carried out. Hank's first job was to prepare the huge crawler tractors and ditch diggers for inspection. This involved hacking and scraping the mud and grime off the exterior of the giant machines. After removing the bulk of this crusted gunge by spade and shovel, Hank finished off with a high-pressure wash. Mac closely supervised this final operation at first; water in its liquid form was an expensive commodity.

"The outside temperature is well below freezing except for a few hours around midday, so all water has to be melted from the ice that surrounds us, and this uses fuel which costs money, do you understand?" Mac was proud of his reputation for economy so he made sure that Hank was fully aware of his point-of-view in very positive terms.

Privately, Mac was well satisfied with the speed with which Hank had adapted to what was required of him. For his part Hank, contrary to his first thoughts when he was told what his work was to be and what was expected of him, soon obtained a sense of satisfaction as the bright paintwork of the tractor appeared from beneath the grime that had covered it. He found that the mud had protected the paint and to see his efforts rewarded with the rich colours of the original condition of these giant machines gave him a pleasant glow of achievement.

One evening in the dining room, as Hank was carefully clearing his dish that had recently been piled high with bacon steaks, beans and hash browns, Mac brought over his own meal and sat down opposite. "How are you settling in?" he enquired. He spoke easily with everyone in the camp and always listened to what was said to him. He soon gained Hank's confidence and smiled as Hank spoke of his satisfaction with his work.

CHAPTER EIGHT

However, Mac's smile faded when Hank commented that he had this problem. Hank said, "I was at a loose end yesterday, towards the end of the shift, so I thought I would straighten the containers in the fuel store; after taking several empty drums to the disposal ditch, I noticed a fine jet of kerosene coming from the back of one of the drums."

"What did you do?" Mac enquired quietly.

Hank hesitated. "Well, I don't seem to hit it off with Dunster, the workshop manager; I felt sure he would yell at me if I said anything so I stuck some of the mud that takes me ages to shift from the scrapers, over the hole. But I'm worried—something seems odd about it and I'm not sure what I should do!"

"Well, you've done the right thing now," Mac assured him. "I'll sort things out. Don't say anything to anyone else, understand?" Hank nodded.

"Transpipe" base camp was ten kilometres east of Anchorage; in the early evening of a bitterly cold day with scurries of snow beating against the triple-glazed window of his office, the project manager MacGreggor was deep in conversation with a massive hulk of a man with a craggy face covered with curly red hair who went by the name of Pete Morgan. Mac was saying, "It looks as if we might be in early this time Pete." Pete Morgan, founder of Morgan Security, nodded affirmation before saying, "We'll need to be careful not to show that we suspect anything."

"I've been thinking about that," replied Mac. "Tomorrow morning you get out of uniform, slip an overall on and a Parka to cover that red thatch of yours, and then wheel a drum trolley into the store. I'll be there for a tour of inspection and will see that no one disturbs you while you have a good look around. If it's what we think you can set up the sensor and warning system."

The following evening Pete reported to Mac. "It's a cute dodge, Mac; young Hank apparently didn't notice that the jet was hitting a power line junction box; and although all power equipment is the double seal type and normally very safe, if the lid has been removed and then replaced loosely without remaking the seal, a squirt of kerosene on it and hey presto, you have all the makings of a fire bomb; all that's missing is a precise timer. Sooner or later the liquid will cause a short across the conductors and then it's bonfire night!" The two men talked at length but came up with no prospective culprit. It was a harassing period; there had been several so-called accidents recently. Only two days previously the jib of a two hundred tonne crane had crashed, causing three fatalities and damage to surrounding equipment. Mac was tormented at having to place the operator onto other duties; the man was a long serving and reliable crane operator but could offer no explanation for the tragedy, and as no mechanical fault was found, a sacrifice was expected and Mac reluctantly had to provide one. So Mac was glad of the opportunity to wait with Pete that night for a signal from the detection unit that had been hidden in the fuel store. "Unless he smells a rat, he's bound to check his set up," Pete said. "This could be the biggest blow he has yet made."

It was a long night; the two men took turns to catnap but anticipation of action prevented anything more than a pretence of sleep. Just after three a.m. the radio controlled buzzer indicated movement in the fuel store. Pete Morgan immediately contacted the five guards he had earlier briefed on what to expect.

"You know what to do!" he barked.

These men hurried to their prearranged positions. Mac and Pete raced to the workshop. Here they found the personnel door closed but unlocked; they quietly let themselves through, closing the door after them. Inside, low-powered night-lights dimly lit the building. They made their way toward the fuel store. Suddenly they were aware of an orange glow at the far end of the building.

"Fire!" gasped Pete!

"Hit the fire alarm!" yelled Mac. "But we've got to find this crackpot before all else." Mac ignored the fire, which was growing rapidly; he ignored the fire alarm that hooted in his ears and the shouts from outside. The dim lights provided poor visibility in the workshop and Mac concentrated on the most important component of the night's vigil...

Where was the fire raiser? Pete Morgan had started the fire alarm howling; now he too was looking for the cause of the fire. He carefully kept himself out of sight, hiding between the giant machines that dominated the workshop. He found himself at the end of a line of trucks, which were on his left hand; on his right were three enormous scrapers. As he slowly made his way up this corridor he heard the grating of a starter motor. A moment later he was dazzled as powerful headlights poured down on him. A deep throated roar as the engine was revved to full power drowned his senses; it added to the howl of the fire siren causing Pete to hesitate as his mind, confused by the thought-destroying noise, raced to try to understand what was happening.

One fact quickly established priority; the brilliant lights like a dragon's eyes were heading directly towards him and getting closer; the engine was screaming, the noise was mind-numbing.

Pete turned to retreat the way he had come but his eyes were full of red and green stars; he lost his sense of direction. As he fumbled vaguely for a gap in the line of machines that formed the corridor he was trapped in, he stumbled; his head struck a solid metal plate and he collapsed to the floor where he lay dazed.

The screaming tractor with the baleful lights was very close but Pete was too numb to move. He knew that he must pull himself to one side. His brain told him that there must be space beneath one of the trucks but it didn't tell him which side to head for and it didn't help his legs to move. A dazed Pete thought, "I must have been looking in the right direction; he saw me coming and is now driving straight at me! If I can just get under one of these trucks I'm safe." The fact that his mind was functioning didn't improve his muscle co-ordination; his legs simply refused to do more than help him stagger a few more steps before he collapsed again. The crawler tractor was advancing straight down the corridor of equipment; there was no driver; the tractor would run straight until one of the tracks was braked to cause a change of direction. Pete lay helpless in its path.

Mac had made his way to the centre of the building and

was looking carefully around when he heard the tractor engine fire up. He saw a figure leap from the driving cab and run away from him, and he immediately gave chase. As he raced behind the tractor he glanced sideways and in the bright headlights he saw Pete stumble and fall. So intent was he on catching the figure he was pursuing that the significance of what he saw was slow to register.

Then the full horror of the situation became clear; it took him valuable seconds to check his headlong chase; then wheeling around he spurted after the roaring tractor. It didn't take long to come up to the cab doorway; the door was swinging backwards and forwards. The normal method of entry was to step onto the track and then into the cab. But there was no recognised way of entering when the tracks were in motion. Mac realised that there was little time left before this roaring monster crushed Pete to pulp. Not waiting to consider his own potential fate if his foot became trapped in the moving tracks, he leaped for the doorway. His right boot stamping down hard onto the moving track gave him leverage to launch himself head first into the cab.   He   landed painfully, his stomach making violent contact with the metal-framed seat. His hands were groping desperately for a grip to pull him fully in and away from the hazard of those large toothed tracks. It felt like a lifetime but somehow he managed to pull himself upright onto the driving seat and then stamp urgently with both feet onto the brake pedals. The tractor stopped dead.

Mac was thrown head first into the windscreen; he saw stars, yet he managed to retain sufficient control of his senses to keep the brakes firmly on. Now the pain in his stomach was an unforgiving agony; he could feel himself gradually slipping into unconsciousness; the pressure on the brake-pedals faltered, the tractor lunged forward once more hesitantly. Pete was slowly clambering to his knees.

Then a hand came into the cab and pulled the compression release; the roaring engine died into silence. Mac sank back into the seat. The pain in his stomach was unbearable; his sense of purpose gave out. The security guard who had stopped the engine was calling for help. Pete Morgan finally struggled to his feet to poke his head over the dozer blade. "Have you caught him?" he gasped. It was some time later that the fate so narrowly escaped finally caught up with him and put Pete into bed in the base sick bay next to Mac—where both men became...

"The worst patients I've ever had to deal with!" snapped the formidable nursing sister in charge. The two men were the only casualties of the night's activities. The fire was contained with minimal damage and the culprit was caught trying to escape from the rear of the building.

Soloman Dunster grinned with savage delight as he twisted the throttle control to maximum and thought, "Now I'll get even with Pete Morgan." He'd never got on with the big security boss; he would never forgive him for poking his nose into the little sideline in hydraulic fluid he'd had going. Although nothing had ever been proved, the questioning had forced him to curtail his operating fiddle for a while. And Soloman Dunster needed all the extra cash that he could lay hands on. The thought of killing two birds with one stone amused him even in his present difficult position; a runaway tractor in the workshop was bound to attract sufficient attention to allow him to get out unnoticed and if Pete

Morgan went under at the same time, so much the better. These thoughts had run through Soloman Dunster's mind as he leapt from the roaring tractor and headed for the small door at the rear of the building. He slipped through the opening, looked around and was moving toward the dormitory block; he took no more than ten paces when a brilliant flashlight hit him full in the face.

"Stop or I fire!" barked the man behind the light.

Dunster shouted back, "Get out of my way you fool, can't you see there's a fire in there? I'm going to fetch help."

"Not so fast, Bud!" snarled another voice in his ear, "You're coming with us." Notwithstanding his angry and increasingly desperate protestations of the need for him to fight the fire, the two guards, in accordance with their instructions, hurried him to the security office. With his entry into the H.Q. Dunster seemed to collapse; his confident bombast left him and he slumped into a chair and cried, "For God's sake gimme a drink!"

The other occupants all stared at him; any form of intoxicants was strictly forbidden in a camp like this. However, Dunster became so distraught, half crying, half shouting, that eventually the camp doctor had to give him a sedative to quieten him down.

Then, as if he had to talk, the whole story came tumbling out; how he had expected to be offered the camp manager's job and instead he only got the servicing side. His gambling debts had caught up with him; he was being pressed for money by hard-nosed credit-collectors. As he fell further behind they increased the interest rate so that he fell deeper and deeper into debt; he needed more and more just to stand still. "If I could cause enough damage to MacGreggor's reputation," he said, "I might still get the top job and the extra pay would get me straight." And that was the gist of the report that Mac and Pete received the next day in the sick bay where they were still confined, fratching and complaining, impatient for release.

Henceforth the work progressed smoothly...

Hank, whose observation had first drawn Mac's notice to the potential firebomb, became increasingly useful around the camp. Mac found it convenient to send him on errands in connection with the many and diverse activities he administered. Hank kept his eyes open and became knowledgeable about the many aspects of this huge undertaking; subsequently through his natural curiosity and intelligence, he was able to pass on to Mac his acute observations.

"It's like having an extra pair of eyes," thought Mac.

This was the start of a strange relationship; Mac the tough experienced forty-year-old, and Hank the young greenhorn who over the next two years which the contract took to complete, became Mac's right hand.

Mac thought about the day that young Hank had first approached him asking for work; it was difficult for him to recall his feelings so long ago and he uneasily reviewed once more his apprehension that so many aspects of this present job raised in his mind!

It took three days and nights, with all the blowers running at full power, to get just a flabby outline of the structure; then a further 24 hours, to build up sufficient pressure to carry the load about to be imposed. With the exception of Hank and a very limited core of specialists, Mac was not allowed to bring in any manpower of his own choosing. He was furious when he became aware of the restrictions on staffing; he was used to running a project from start to finish, but the terms of employment were extremely generous in all other respects and he developed an overriding curiosity about the nature of this unusual building-work that had been hinted at and his contract clearly stated that once signed there would be no release until the project was completed. Although few of the workforce supplied to him had any construction experience, mixing and applying concrete is a simple task mainly requiring a strong back. So he had few grounds for complaint on that score; he was awed by the level of intelligence displayed and, once instructed, very little repeat explanation was necessary; but what were such people doing here on a building site in the middle of a desert?

Mac and Hank drove over to the concrete production unit where Buz Obas, the giant chemical engineer in charge of the plant, grinned down at the diminutive figure of Mac.

"Ready whenever you give the word, Bossman."

It amused Obas to pretend that he was taking orders from Mac.

Black as pitch, Buz Obas was almost two metres tall and had a string of qualifications as long as his brawny arms; he always appeared to be bubbling over with good humour and never let up with the banter and jest.

"We've got the aggregate plant popping like popcorn; I've just checked the chemical analysis of our latest test mix and it comes to 99% of specification."

"Why is it different to the mix you used for the foundation?" asked a curious Hank.

Buz took a deep breath and with an elaborate sigh said, "For the upper structure we need the material as light as we can get it to reduce the weight on the foundations and to avoid the need for reinforcement.

"So-oo, instead of using the sand as it comes, we cook it; now the fun begins. If we simply heated sand we would finish up with glass and we're not going to make a big glass house; think of how hot you guys would be working in that. So we have devised a technique that first melts the outside of each individual grain of sand; we allow that to cool a little, then just as the itty-bitty particle thinks we have finished with him we give him a quick burst of microwave energy; this heats up the centre and causes expansion; the outer surface is still soft enough to allow this, so we end up with a hollow particle of sand. Cool these before they land in the collecting hopper and we have a very light aggregate that has more than double the volume of normal sand. However, the cooking changes the chemical composition, so I have to modify the recipe."

Then serious for a moment, Obas continued, "We are still getting quality variations in the cement supply, Mac. We need a better person up there at the cement plant."

"Okay," Mac replied drearily, "I'll get a report off to H.Q."

This was the part of his job that Mac hated; he had no control over personnel, and that this relieved him of responsibility was no satisfaction. His way would be to go straight up to the plant, kick a few arses and if that didn't work replace the top man. But today all he could say was a pathetic, "I'll report it to H.Q."

Mac was in no mood for talking, so it was a silent journey back to the campsite; here a fresh convoy of supplies had just arrived. Mac and Hank were kept busy arranging for the orderly storage of the multitudinous materials.

Next morning, Hank was up and out of his tent early; he

was anxious to see how the concreting would go. The first team was already starting when the concrete arrived; a pipe was pushed into the hopper of the truck, the concrete was sucked out and delivered to a rapidly revolving spiral mixer. An emulsifying agent and air under pressure were incorporated at this stage, and then the aerated buoyant mass was blown through a large nozzle pipe directly onto the inflated membrane former of the building.

Application was rapid, the load soon gone.

"It's just like sloshing rice pudding onto the wall of your bedroom!" yelled the excited young man on the nozzle.

Hank thinking of his father's voice, if ever he were to be guilty of such a thing, wondered what sort of home the young man had been reared in.

However, he had little time to consider the point; it was just another insight into the peculiar attitudes of these people that he was working with. The concrete truck was empty now; Hank's next job was to calculate the time taken, and then contact Buz Obas at the mixing plant so that a supply schedule could be worked out. The timing would be critical; this concrete was fast cure and the last thing wanted was for a load to harden in one of the trucks.

Hank soon found a new problem to tax his mind; examining the first area covered he found wide variations in the thickness of the coating. There was no skilled labour here and just sloshing the stuff on regardless of a uniform thickness was not acceptable.

"The spec calls for .3 metre," he said.

The laughing faces round him fell silent; empty of suggestion!

Talking over the day's events with Mac in the mess tent

later that day, Hank was going on to the next problem when Mac interrupted. "How did you deal with the thickness business?"

"Oh, I remembered that the tent pegs we use are about the right length, so I've arranged to insert them at regular intervals to act as depth gauges."

"That's a good idea son; I wonder what they'll think at H.Q. when they get a requisition in for half a million tent pegs?"

Mac smiled; he liked the idea of upsetting H.Q.—it helped him to overcome his frustration at having to work with unskilled labour. But he liked better the confident manner in which Hank dealt with the many daily situations that normally would have been referred to himself. He temporarily forgot his worries about the peculiarities that abounded on this project and persuaded himself that it was an inspiration that had led him to bring Hank with him to his latest undertaking.

CHAPTER NINE

The third and final meeting of the founding members of Project Pegasus was held at the temporary H.Q. on Hainan Island. I opened the proceedings with a report on progress made at the Base camp.

"The Igloo is completed externally; now internal floor levels are being built. Here is problem number one: we're desperately in need of skilled building labour, and I feel it essential to take on some outside contractors to enable us to finish the building within a reasonable time period. We are recruiting our own people rapidly and it's proving difficult to find suitable occupations for all the new entrants." Ched interrupted to say, "I'll not be able to keep the lid on the anti-grav business for much longer. I've received formal notice from the governors, that they want a full report on Flux 59, the code name that we've been using. I'll have to make a complete statement on progress so far and if the implications are not already obvious as I suspect, it won't be long before we have the entire scientific world breathing down our necks, panting for everything we know. In any case we've finished all the major calculations; it's time we started on the practical side of things."

There was a short pause; then Lin Ho, in her delightfully musical accent, said, "During the course of our screening procedures we have had to reject several candidates for the project on grounds of potential instability in an unknown environment; could we not include suitable people as an additional group, a support group? People who would not actually accompany the expedition? Now that we have an isolated base to work from surely we can maintain our security with a completely sealed site?"

There followed several excited proposals from other members of the party. Teng Ho thought that help would be forthcoming from Chinese Army Engineers. Ched suggested engineering students from his institute; there were many variations along these lines. Eventually it was agreed that as the site engineer, MacGreggor was proving to be so competent he should be allowed to recruit his own staff—as he had wished to do all along. This would be conditional on there being no outside leave for the duration of the scheme.

I commented, "At least I might get him off my back and stop his sarcastic requests for half a million tent pegs and additional towels to dry behind the ears of the people he has to work with at present."

Finally a name and an opening date were set.

Project Pegasus would officially open for business in the heart of the Sinkian desert forty-five days from the present time, i.e., July 1st, 2151.

The remaining business was quickly concluded; now that a definite date was set, all members were anxious to be away to make their own final arrangements.

Ched and Eva returned to California in the private plane that went with his position of Dean. They were alone, sitting comfortably in the luxurious cabin. The stewardess was up front chatting with the pilots in the cockpit. Ched was saying,

"There's ten of them to get out; they all have partners, so that makes twenty. We can start with the Paris convention. I can't send more than four observers; even that will raise eyebrows. I've managed to keep them away from everything for over three years now. Then Si Lucas can take compassionate leave; he told me last week that his mother is very near to the end of her life; they have always been close but at least her death will remove any hesitation about leaving which Si may have been prone too.   Do you think that you could coach Ben Hoyt in how to imitate a nervous breakdown? If we could swing that, it shouldn't be difficult to get him a passage on a convalescent liner with his wife as nurse." Ched was in his element making arrangements like this.

"So then we'll be into summer break with the final four to cook up outlandish areas to visit for their vacations. That should keep our watching busy-bodies occupied. I'll leave my notice of abdication to the last day of term; the board will be annoyed but if all goes well we won't have to worry about that anyway."

A few days later a birthday party for the youngest member of the anti-grav group afforded Ched an opportunity to inform the whole team of the adventure which lay ahead. As he had expected, there was intense excitement with this news. Afterwards he wondered, "Will there be any fallouts?" He had spelt out very clearly that they had just over a month to make their final farewells to all they knew or loved on earth. He had impressed the need for secrecy on everyone but deep inside his heart, he had grave doubts of being able to depend on 100% success. He refused to worry; he knew that he had done his best, and he had already completed arrangements for the four Physicists to attend the Paris conference. During the course of the party Ben had a long discussion with Eva. This was unusual and caused a few questioning looks. However, when Ben suddenly exploded two days later and threw a flask of liquid Nitrogen at one of the lab assistants, apparently nobody connected the two unusual incidents. So successful was this camouflage that most of the team were genuinely surprised to meet Ben at Pegasus, only six weeks later.

Meanwhile back at the temporary H.Q. on Hainan island news of a near disaster was been described; I was appalled, to be immediately followed with apprehension listening to the report of Dr Stronberg.

"You must realise sir, we have the strictest specification to adhere to. When the psychiatrists have passed the recruits, we have to ensure as far as humanly possible that they are physically fit both now and as far as we can ascertain for the future.

"There is a radiation booth, which has been in common use for many years. Its normal purpose is to sterilise the exterior of staff before entering the clean rooms of biological or electronic laboratories. We decided that as we were in effect staffing a completely new and isolated community, this was an opportunity to eliminate all the normal bacteria that share our world with us. So we installed two of the latest models at the entrance of Pegasus.

"All new personnel are told about the booths. They don't need to undress. The irradiation level is set at two minutes."

"Yes, yes, yes," I exclaimed, "please get on with it."

Dr Stronberg took a deep breath and continued, "One minute and thirty five seconds after Hussain Walit entered the radiation booth, he exploded! The explosion was sufficient to cause considerable damage to the reception area; it killed the radiologist on duty and two other new recruits waiting to go through."

"Yes," I said, "I know all that; what I need to know is the cause, and if we're likely to suffer a recurrence." Dr Stronberg took another deep breath and continued, "Hussain Walit had a wife who was with the new female recruits, and she was outside the reception building but was amongst the first to enter after the explosion. As you will realise, no one knew what had happened for a while; but as the sequence of events gradually became clear, Hussain Rosendy suddenly collapsed with a moaning cry and started tearing at the clothes around her stomach; she was rolling on the floor screaming, 'Get it out, get it out!'

"Medics were all around and they quickly gave her a tranquillising shot and got her to sick bay. It was then that the story began to unfold: She told the doctor that she was carrying explosives in her womb. She was mostly incoherent, but insistent that the doctor remove the container immediately. You can imagine the doctor's dilemma! The entire base had heard the explosion, and here was another walking bomb!

"Although it was suggested, we couldn't just turn her out into the desert.

"The sick bay is only a temporary tent and finally Dr Migalov, who I must commend for his courage, with two qualified helpers decided to examine Hussain Rosendy under a general anaesthetic and in effect, performed a caesarean section to deliver a parcel of detonators!

"Eventually we collected enough remnants of Hussain Walit to arrive at a possible explanation. His wife told us that they were both recruited to carry out as much damage to the project as possible. Their payment would be graded to the amount of damage they caused. The payment was to be made to their parents who were still living in squalid conditions in a poor area and significantly, would be made whether or not they survived. It seems that Hussain had swallowed, probably with the help of Hypno-anasthesia, several packets of a new type of explosive. These were contained in a sausage-like sheath; they had been instructed to eat large amounts of protein food to mask the contents from X-ray examination. The food they chose was smoked fish and pickled walnuts; these in combination form uric acid, and it seems likely that this acid eroded the container and stimulation by the radiation reacted with the explosive."

Ro said, "Thank you, doctor. If you can add nothing more please return to your duties."

The new base was now operational but as we were still short of recruits, I remained on Hainan at the temporary H.Q. I now realised that security for Pegasus had reached a new and urgent phase. I called an emergency meeting of the original band of friends who were in effect the Pegasus Project Executive. They all knew what had occurred; so I opened the proceedings by saying, "We are suffering increasingly determined efforts to infiltrate Pegasus; we seem to be effectively screening out obvious spies. However, this recent episode demonstrates that we are benefiting from a degree of luck and we cannot rule out the possibility that we have missed one or two others. Apart from constant vigilance in our daily work I don't see what else we can do. But it would be short-sighted not to expect external aggression also, so I would like to hear your views on how best to deal with the situation."

There was no rush of suggestions. At last Ched said

doubtfully, "There's a chance that the anti-grav device could be developed into a form that could become a giant magnet, that could possibly pull planes down to earth; but I'm reluctant to divert any effort from the main objective."

No one spoke for several minutes, until Oval Himnal said quietly, "With limited help and facilities, I can solve the problem of external hostile opposition! I know of work that was started and never concluded that will produce a mind-destroying beam of particles; a beam that will shatter any brain in its path! The range is indefinite and needs exploring, as does the focusing. If these difficulties can be solved, we could mount the transmitter on a geostationary satellite and surround the base with a sterilising wall of radiation."

Looks of astonishment and disbelief greeted this calm confident statement.

"How is it that we've heard nothing about this?" questioned several sceptical voices at once. "How can you be so sure of your facts?"

Oval continued, "You have not heard of the Death Ray, because it was discovered by chance and early development work was carried out by two physicists straight out of university where they came across the principles accidentally. They continued the work completely within their own resources; it was because of the horror they felt for their discovery that they spoke to no one at all about it. The electronics involved are commonplace; they needed no great funding or equipment to continue their investigation. The mistake they made was trying to keep the secret to themselves; they were forced into basic bad practice when it came to testing the apparatus.

"When looking for suitable testing sites because of the

curvature of the earth, they needed a position high enough to give a clear line of sight in excess of 300 km; the only isolated area they could think of was Antarctica. Their idea was for one to set up and operate the transmitter at a fixed known position and the other would take the boat to differing distances to measure signal strength. Communication between the two was by short wave radio; to avoid attention the transmissions were short and limited to brief periods. A method of self-protection had been devised; this took the form of a full head insulating helmet."

Oval's account had her listeners spellbound; all were intent on hearing every syllable of this fascinating tale. A strange air of excitement was emanating from the big blonde woman, which held the whole company in its grip! No one commented about the change in tense when she continued.

"We had a fine spell of weather forecast for the next few days. We were reluctant to start, to gain positive proof of what we knew would be the outcome, but decided that we were never likely to get better conditions; so off we set. The photon-transmitter was not difficult to carry and we were packing a small portable Hydro-generator. I started to make my way to the top of the ice shelf. Gunther set sail for the first test position, which was 100 kilometres out; we were both anxious to conclude the range testing as soon as possible so that we could leave this desolate area. We knew that it would take several hours to get the boat into position even if Gunther could run at maximum revs. I set off across broken lumps of ice covered with loose snow towards the cliffs of the escarpment. I've spent many holidays in Norway, so that the climbing technique with aid of a rocket backpack was no problem. Once on top I checked the height—1200 metres, not bad for two hours' effort. I took a bearing on the boat; it had some way to go before we could carry out the first test. So I spent the waiting period building a rough shelter. I didn't expect to be here more than two days but Antarctic conditions are always uncertain.

"The first test was so satisfactory that we decided in a brief message to go straight into the 300 kilometre test.

"Twenty-four hours later this was concluded and we had confirmation that our discovery, a totally new concept of transmitting a form of energy over apparently unlimited distance with negligible transmission loss, was feasible. Gunther expected to return to pick me up the following day; I spent another lonely night in my shelter, then made a leisurely descent to the coastal plain. You will realise that there was no landing for the boat to tie up to. The sea was choppy and I was actually standing on an ice floe. I'd thrown most of my equipment into the boat but when it came to the energy transmitter and the power generator we waited for an opportunity to pass this from hand to hand. The boat with its engine at minimum revs was pushing slowly into the pack ice. As I was handing the transmitter over, the boat suddenly broke into a patch of slush and I was pushed down onto the ice. The power generator fell into the sea; the connections to the transmitter broke loose from the terminals on the generator. The earthing effect of contact with the water triggered a power impulse from the capacitors in the photon-transmitter; it lasted for a millisecond only, but it was enough; Gunther was in the boat with no helmet on; he screamed and fell to the deck. I was on the ice two metres below and out of danger; I eventually scrambled aboard but there was nothing to be done. Gunther, my husband of less than a year, was dead!

"I returned to New Zealand to report Gunther lost at sea. The officer who logged the event was unsympathetic; he told me that inexperienced people should have more sense than to go into dangerous waters."

Tears were now streaming down Oval's cheeks; there was silence among her listeners as each thought of the implications of what they had just heard. Then Beth and Lin Ho rushed over to throw their arms round Oval's shoulders, who now broke down into loud gasping sobs. She had kept the whole story to herself for almost three years, unable to confide in anyone. She was now able to release a torrent of pent-up emotion. There was a break in the proceedings as the girls tried to comfort Oval. The rest of us excitedly discussed the fantastic possibilities of this revelation.

Later I called for order, speaking with the authority I was increasingly being offered. "I'm sure that we all agree that this—for want of a more precise definition, Death Ray—of Oval's should be pursued and if possible developed along the lines she has already suggested."

CHAPTER TEN

Progress at Pegasus base moved smoothly into a higher level of efficiency. MacGreggor was authorised to bring in people of his own choosing. These were people with whom he had worked previously and was confident in their abilities. He nominated Pete Morgan as being an experienced professional who could institute security to the project. This fresh input to key positions meant that he could cope more easily with the enthusiastic but untrained majority of his labour force. The unskilled new recruits were rapidly increasing and soon the interior of the Igloo began to take shape and provided some occupation for them. There were to be six floor levels, approximately twelve metres high; this would still leave sufficient space on top for a helicopter landing area. It was necessary to bring in some constructional   steelwork but the bulk of the building was still to be concrete. The cement production unit in the foothills of the Charmen Tahg Mountains was situated within easy supply distance of the limestone, shale, and methane, which were its raw materials. The Chinese Army which also constructed some meaningless fortifications to provide a cover for the activity operated the plant nominally. But the bulk of the output was spirited away by underground pipeline to Pegasus, which had an insatiable appetite. Here it was converted into standard size load-bearing stanchions, lightweight-flooring beams and finally hollow partitioning. Concrete by the hundreds of tonnes; enough to build a second great wall, according to Buz Obas.

The greatest demand was for workshop facilities and associated laboratories so the furnishing of the first one at ground level started as soon as floor one was completed. The first workshop was a high tech foundry; this would be necessary to provide the hundreds of precision castings that would be required.

The labs ranged from Physics, Metallurgy and Chemistry to Hydraulics and Communications; alongside were many other skills and sciences needing accommodation, to cover the wide range of interests of this project. Most materials were brought in by helicopter; but unusually large or heavy items came by land train, the nearest railhead being at Suchoo 500 kilometres from Pegasus; MacGreggor had helicoptered out to the end of the line to supervise the work. The big containers were fitted with skirts, then with a tractor fore and aft which supplied steerage and air under pressure to lift the load; the train started. This was a very slow business requiring a reasonably flat surface; fifteen km each day was the average distance covered, even with the unlimited manpower of the Chinese Army engineers. They struggled all daylight hours over sand and mud, rocky outcrops and paddy fields. When the giant power generator arrived at Pegasus the container was steered directly into position onto massive foundations and allowed to settle.

The power unit stood outside of the Igloo, and a building was now constructed around it and completely sealed; then an entrance was made from the inside of the main building. This design was to ensure that entry to such vital apparatus could only be from within the main structure, which aimed to be completely secure.

To obscure the traces of this activity was important and entrusted to the Chinese army.

A prominent feature of the interior of the main building was the steeply angled escape chutes that were added immediately at each floor level. This was a huge building and fast emergency exits were a necessary precaution in case rapid evacuation was ever to be resorted to.

Floor two was earmarked for Reception, Security, Communications and Administration. This reception area was to be the only access to the whole complex and therefore had sophisticated security built in. All personnel had to carry personal identification and newcomers were always expected to pass palm print and retina checks on entering the complex from the outside. The limited access to the building explained the escape chutes that were such a notable feature. At the foot of these chutes was an escape flap, which required a signal from the personal identity badge before it would open.

Ben Hoyt's group were the first cohesive team of scientists to arrive at Pegasus. They were told of the plans for installing their workstation at ground floor and that it would be the first part of the construction to be ready. In the meantime they were expected to pitch in to help with the building work. All went well for a while; but the novelty of hard manual labour quickly passed. Then aching backs and bruised fingers led to Ben with increasing bitterness and sarcasm, regularly accosting Mac, "You told us that our shack would be ready in no time Mac, are we running behind schedule?" Mac's neck turned red.

On a revolutionary project such as this, there could be no

timetable in the normally accepted sense of the word, but any semblance of criticism needled Mac, whether justified or not. He made Hank responsible. "Get those goddammed Californians off my back! Tell them if they move in too soon they are likely to get half a tonne of concrete on their soft heads," growled Mac. A few weeks later the first floor was completed providing a safe cover for the ground floor workshop; after which the California group were allowed to install their own services to their future workplace. This last duty had a calming effect on them. All standard laboratory equipment was already on site awaiting installation, but few scientists were ever given the opportunity to order their own specialist gadgets as was happening now.

Hank was thoroughly enjoying life—he was busy. After Mac he was the most conspicuous person on the base though unlike Mac, he was never without a cheerful smile and a pleasant reply to any request. He was still as eager to learn and enthusiastic to tackle any task, however difficult or unpleasant others apparently found the job or however unpopular it was. Add to this a natural talent for getting on with anyone he came into contact with and no false sense of his own importance; he quickly told people he first met, "I specialised in nothing but please explain what you need and see if I can help."

After an introduction such as this, most individuals were happy to explain how important their particular subject was and how necessary the Carbon N12 was to avoid delay on the project. Hank would offer to assist and by knowing so many other self-important staff members could often short circuit the normal requisite paperwork. He never denied his part in the occasional bloomers that happened and wouldn't point out that he had accepted the store man's confident statement, that Carbon NB6 was the equivalent of Carbon 12. In brief, Hank was fast becoming a manager and what is more, a potential leader. Hank was now twenty-two years old; a tall handsome fair-haired young man who attracted inquiring looks from both men and women wherever he went.

He met Annette Lafarge sitting alone in the mess tent one evening. This in itself was unusual; since becoming widowed by the explosion at the entry screening six weeks previously, the rest of the community made great efforts to see that she was never left by herself. Hank, who had been expecting to meet Mac, jumped at the opportunity to eat his meal in feminine company for a change. They had not been formally introduced and for once Hank lost his easy confidence. He had impulsively made his way to Annette's table with his loaded tray; but when he reached her he hesitated and his voice trembled slightly as he said, "My name's Hank, do you mind if I sit here?" Annette looked up and said, "Of course not, please do."

As Hank seated himself he was suddenly conscious of the huge amount of food on his tray. He lifted a dish of stew in front of him and then a large plate of vegetables, which he added to the dish as soon as there was sufficient space on it. As he reached for a chapatti, he looked up to Annette's face and blushing as he thought he had forgotten how, he mumbled, "I'm starving; I've been outside all day and it's freezing."

"I'm sure you need it," Annette smiled, "I've seen you rushing around several times." Once the ice was broken they soon started talking about their different duties at the site. Annette said, "I started helping in the sick bay, but as things were quiet I offered to help in the canteen." She smiled as she added, "I'm a botanist really but there are as yet no facilities for me here." She had, she said, been in research until the fateful day Pierre came rushing home to say that they had this opportunity to enrol for the most exciting project in a lifetime. "He was so enthusiastic and then everything happened so fast; we were both orphans without family to consider. We resigned from our duties, sold our home, then travelled across the world to Hainan. I've never experienced such an exhaustive interview; we were flown here, to an unknown destination, and I still don't know where we are exactly. Then we were given a detailed medical examination and started to walk towards the radiation booth. Suddenly a violent explosion deafened me and partially blinded all who were close. There was flying sand and debris all over; it caused me only superficial lacerations, but then I was faced with the news that Pierre was dead!"

Tears were now streaming down Annette's cheeks and she sobbed quietly. An embarrassed Hank didn't know what to do or say; fortunately he had finished his meal and was able to offer his large hand across the table between them. Annette accepted his hand, and he experienced a new and totally novel sensation: how pleasant it was to be holding the hands of this tearful dark haired girl who seemed to be deriving comfort from his touch.

CHAPTER ELEVEN

Beth and I, Eva and Ched Taylor, Teng Ho Pot, with his wife Lin Ho, were seated around a table having dinner together one evening. When coffee had been served and we were expecting no further interruptions, we fell to discussing our work, in particular my forthcoming visit to Switzerland. Teng Ho opened with the topic that was uppermost in all our minds.

"If this group from Help Unlimited could find and approach Charlie Stultz while he was in Paris, supposedly playing the part of an observer at the ultra-sonic cruiser conference...." He paused, and added quietly, "but in reality trying to divert his spies from his real intention of heading for China and disappearing; how can anyone connected with the project hope to remain unknown and especially the top man?"

Ched said, "We must all be watched individually. I knew that I was being followed but I'd no idea that the entire team were!"

"So much for secrecy," I grunted.

Teng Ho continued, "Have you considered that this may be a ruse to get Ro out into the open, away from the security that we enjoy here?"

Beth turned pale. "That possibility had never occurred to me. I'd only thought of having to stay here by myself for a few days."

"Do you have to upset Beth?" asked Lin Ho.

Ched spoke quietly, "There's no point in closing our minds to unpleasant possibilities."

"So now perhaps you'll agree to accepting help from Chino security?" said Teng Ho.

"I've already started. I've had an interesting meeting with Jon Chan; he has full responsibility for getting me there and back. Has no one noticed my eyes yet?"

They all looked at me and as they started to exclaim, I quickly said, "Don't shout, it's part of my disguise."

What no one had noticed until their attention had been directed to it was that my distinctive blue eyes were now a muddy brown colour. "It affects my skin pigmentation as well," I went on, "and you should see what it does to my turds."

"Oh Ro," laughed Beth, "Do you have to?"

The reason for all this discussion was an apparently serious enquiry about the possibility of joining the project by several members of the development arm of the mighty "H.U.".

Help unlimited was the most prestigious of the 22nd century successors to what used to be called the White Goods industry. Domestic appliances had gradually developed into primitive robot-like household contraptions. A miniature D.R.A.K.was a refinement that took many years to evolve, but when this was achieved, the "Android" was born! It was still not possible to fit a football sized Drak into the head of an Android, but it was not necessary; there was plenty of room in the chest or stomach areas. A small hydrogen power unit provided unlimited and almost everlasting energy; so the attentive, untiring, unflappable, maid of all work, had arrived.

As for centuries past, the Swiss led the field in the type of intricate mechanism this highly specialised work demanded. Hence the interest by the project's leaders in the possibility of attracting new recruits from such eminent quarters. The opportunities were far too exciting to risk missing; this was the reason for my personal involvement.

One week later Roland Stern boarded the normal internal flight for Beijing. Here he was seen to enter the government compound and was not seen again for several days.

Once inside government buildings, I was taken to Jon Chan who, wasting little time on formalities, took me to be fitted with a wig of long black hair; I was given instruction in how to walk with a stoop and dressed in the current attire of a government inspector; I was then ready to face the world as Chung Peng.

"Now we head for the international airport." From here Jon Chan contacted his office. He nodded in satisfaction as he heard that my watcher was still on station observing my double inside government buildings.

Some hours later, on arrival in Switzerland, we casually made our way to Lausanne on lake Geneva where we played the role of tourists until evening when we were due to contact the party from H.U., Help Unlimited.

This was the group who had known enough about the so-called secret project to approach one of our members to ask for more information.

Jon and I entered the dining room of the "Olympic Restaurant" early. There was only one table occupied, so we had no difficulty finding seats at a table in a corner away from windows. Here we declined to order a meal and had drinks brought to the table. Jon Chan carefully placed the book that we had bought that morning in a prominent position; it was a story about a mythical period in the Earth's early history, when gods and goddesses mingled with the human beings of an early dominant race called Greeks. The title *Odyssey* was clearly visible. We talked quietly together for a while.

"Someone is looking at us," Jon spoke carefully. Sitting with his back to the wall he could see what was happening in the restaurant without appearing too obvious. A few minutes later three youngish men sat at the next table; they gave an order and then the nearest with a glance at the book, spoke to me. "I see that you like fables!"

"We can always learn from the masters," I replied cautiously.

The arranged code had been given and received and in a little while Jon and I joined the three, who introduced themselves as Curt, Herman and Paul. I immediately asked, "What have you to offer?"

"Would you be interested in a Robot that appeared and acted as a human being; can operate for 48 weeks without recharging, can speak and understand any language simply by changing a disk and is twice as strong as any man?"

"A demonstration would help," I smiled. Curt picked up the leather bound book, which lay on the table; he passed it to Paul and looking straight into his eyes said slowly, "I want that book torn into two sections, Paul!" Paul picked up the book, looked at it carefully then effortlessly tore it into two equal pieces.

"If you wish to repeat those instructions in Mandarin, Paul is at present programmed in English, German and in honour of your visit, in classical Chinese." Curt returned the two halves of the torn book to me and, after a quick glance, I passed them onto Jon.

"We have not yet got around the problem of pretending to eat," said Curt. "As it isn't obvious that he is not drinking, I suggest I take him out and return with the real Paul to continue our business." Curt and Paul stood up and walked out of the restaurant; five minutes later what appeared to be the same two men returned and took their places at the table; we then commenced to eat and talk. The three Swiss explained how they formed one of many development groups that worked for H.U. on a freelance basis. "We are responsible for the 'Psychical' brain—the component that makes Paul's robotic double into an Android. Surely appliances such as we have demonstrated would prove invaluable for the scheme you are working on?" Curt said.

"That leads me to ask, how did you know about us?" I queried.

"The whole scientific world knows that something is afoot," smiled Curt. "We discussed the matter between ourselves for a while; then applied our minds to who was likely to be involved. We came up with Ched Taylor as the most promising choice and when we found out that a group of his people were making an unaccustomed appearance in Europe, we felt sure something was about to happen. So we put out feelers, and sure enough, a week later fifty scientists and mathematicians disappeared and you wouldn't be here if we weren't on the right track."

I knew only too well how researchers talk to each other; whatever their respective employers or governments may decree to the contrary.

"Have you considered leaving everything here behind you forever?" I questioned sombrely.

"We have become a self-contained unit," stated Curt levelly. "We have worked and lived together for several years now. We have no other ties." He looked at me with a slight smile on his lips, his eyebrows lifting in an interrogating gesture.

"I understand," I replied quietly.

The conversation continued until the meal was over, with questions and answers on both sides; we then agreed to meet again the following evening and went our separate ways.

Jon and I walked slowly back towards our hotel talking over what had been said. "I hope that I never have to try putting an arm lock on that robot," Jon was saying; he would have continued but we were accosted by two attractive girls. "How about two good looking fellahs taking my sister and me home?" smiled the taller of the two looking directly at me. I returned the smile, "Not tonight girls, thank you." Jon and I made to walk on. "Aw come on fellahs, we're very nice when you get to know us." We continued walking; the girls persisted for a little longer, but as the hotel with its brightly illuminated forecourt and security guards drew near they retired. As we entered the foyer, Jon speaking calmly, said, "I think that we've been spotted; that was no ordinary attempted pick up— they were too persistent; there's plenty of business around here for them. I'm sure we were marked down for special attention. The question is, what happens now?"

I left Jon to collect the room key. As the escalator deposited us at floor twenty-five, Jon looked carefully up and down the corridor. Nobody was in sight. "That's interesting." Where was the floor security guard? The door to the floor hostess's room was also closed. "Okay, let's go."

As we reached our apartment, Jon took a small tube from his inside pocket and, softly placing one end against the door, put his ear to the other. After a few moments he smiled gently; then with a gesture to me to keep back, he inserted the key card into the door lock, pushed the door open wide and sprang quickly into the room.

As Jon entered his eyes swept the room, darting into all corners; then he crouched and went into a forward roll that took him into the centre of the floor. As he jumped up the pen-like object he held in his hand spat a jet of smoke into the face of one of the two figures that were waiting. The figure instantly collapsed.

The second figure, though surprised, reacted in a flash to strike a savage blow at Jon's neck, but though it landed on its target Jon was already moving forward again. Never stay still for a moment, was the instructions from his early training for the acrobat team he had expected to join. The blow, which would have pole-axed him had he been stationary, merely helped him on his way to his next position, which was immediately in front of the window. When his adversary threw his second vicious punch at Jon's head, Jon ducked and then head-butted the man in the stomach. The man's fist went straight through the glass, showering splinters inside and out. Jon's attack had pushed his legs from under him so that he sprawled face down on the floor; his right wrist bleeding and leaving a trail of blood down the wall.

Jon rolled to one side and quickly assumed his semi-crouched position while making another swift appraisal of the situation; satisfied there were not many hiding places in a hotel room, he motioned me in with a wave of his hand. After a quick glance into the bathroom, he shot the lock as he closed the door. "I don't expect to get any useful information out of this dog," he said, indicating the man climbing up from the floor; the man was darting anxious glances from belligerent eyes, looking around, trying to decide his next move. "So I'll keep him quiet." With these words Jon pointed the tube at the man and again a sharp crack accompanied by a jet of smoke struck the man's head. The effect was immediate: the man crumpled into unconsciousness. "He will remain so for at least two hours," Jon answered my questioning look.

We considered our position and decided that we were unlikely to be disturbed again that night; so Jon made a slight adjustment to his weapon and using it like a hypodermic, shot a dose of narcotic directly into each body that lay on the floor.

"That will keep them out of our hair for twelve hours." He attached a miniature sensor to the bedroom door saying, "The slightest vibration will trigger an alarm; now we can have a good night's sleep and decide our next moves tomorrow."

I lay awake for a little while thinking over the day's events; I had been careful to appear neutral about the three scientists' disclosures, but beneath my calm exterior I was extremely excited at the obvious prospects opened up by the information that we had been given. Intelligent robots could save months of time-consuming safety testing. To be able to test theories without having to devise techniques to avoid risking human life was just the first benefit to jump into my thoughts. This was followed immediately by wondering how we were to return to our Chinese base of operations now that we had been discovered, and with three effeminate additions. Although our talks had not been finalised, I was determined to take the three men so recently met with us.

I could be very determined when I'd decided on a course of action.

There was no point in worrying about how we had been discovered; I had no time to regret what was done; the future was far more interesting.

CHAPTER TWELVE

The following morning I ordered breakfast to be brought to our room. I met the food trolley in the corridor, then wheeled the breakfast into the room, carefully locking the door behind me. I addressed Jon, "I imagine that we'll need at least twenty-four hours to make alternative arrangements. Can we do it?" Jon lifted the mattress off the base of one of the twin beds. "Look," he said, "these bases are only a sparsely sprung frame. If we cut through the top cover and remove a few springs we could easily fit a man inside." So after eating a good English breakfast ("None of this continental style eating for me, thank you!") we proceeded to hack a body-sized hole into each bed base; then lifting both unconscious bodies into them, we replaced the mattresses.

"That's made the place look better, but we can't risk the staff coming in to clean the room so we'll have to remain here all day. I wish we had arranged to meet earlier than this evening."

"It could be worse," said Jon. "Whoever is looking for us will know that we're still here. There's too much servicing activity taking place during the day for them to try a frontal attack. All the cleaning monitors are equipped with cameras, which give full surveillance of each floor, so I don't expect any trouble until tonight. I've been thinking about how we must leave without being stopped, but we won't be able to carry cases."

I contacted reception and ordered a taxi for the following morning—"to give our watchers something to think about." We then settled down to a long, weary day of waiting. To help pass the time we exchanged stories of our previous occupations. Jon told of his early life and of his memories of his mother and father. He recounted his sad story of when he was a child in a touring circus troupe, which travelled between villages and small towns on the northern borders of China. One dreadful night Mongolian brigands attacked their encampment on the outskirts of the hamlet they had arrived at. "My mother was carried away in the raid. As soon as it was daylight my father set off in pursuit. He never returned alive! Two days later his headless body was dumped at the circus site."

Jon was adopted by a family of tumblers who trained him to earn a living as they did. His quiet voice grated with emotion as he continued, "I stayed with the circus until I was eighteen, and then I joined the police force. My one ambition is to come up against the bastards who abducted and killed my parents."

Evening came at last; twenty minutes before the time that we had arranged to meet Curt and friends, we cautiously let ourselves out of the room.

"There's bound to be someone waiting," said Jon; and so it proved, but just as effectively as last night, Jon disabled our first adversary and I, who was purposely walking backwards close behind, did the same to the two other aspiring assailants who appeared from one of the bedrooms from which they had been watching all passers-by. "I feel like an old time gunfighter," I laughed, with a projector in each hand as Jon and I raced down the corridor to the fire escape. It took Jon less than two minutes to circumvent the security system on the door to open air. We reached ground level without further incident and casually strolled to our rendezvous. Curt, Herman and Paul were waiting as arranged.

While we were having drinks, Curt said, "We own a hover cruiser in which we spend our leisure periods. I suggest that we use our transporter to go out to the lake and hold our meeting on board. We could take her out a little way to ensure privacy."

"That's an excellent idea," I responded.

I automatically nodded "Good evening" to the figure seated in the rear seat before realising that I was greeting Paul's double. The robot however calmly replied, "Good evening Chung Peng, good evening, Jon Chan."

Less than an hour later Jon and I were admiring the beautiful lines of an ocean-going cruiser which was lying docile and elegant at her moorings of the yacht club.

"She's the most beautiful boat I've ever seen," I said admiringly. This tribute was well received by the three owners. They were obviously proud of their craft and happy to receive complimentary remarks about her. We all boarded and the vessel purred away from her resting place and onto the broad waters of Lake Geneva. As we drew away from the shore, both Jon and I kept a sharp lookout for any evidence of having attracted attention or of being followed. We had not disclosed our adventures of the previous twenty-four hours to the others, but were very much aware of the danger that we were in. A few miles offshore Curt instructed the robot to follow a slow figure of eight cruising pattern. "He's quite capable of that," smiled Curt to me, "and if anything unusual occurs he'll let us know." With that remark Curt led the way to the large well-appointed saloon. There we all started into the sandwiches and coffee, which had been brought, and followed our meal with innumerable questions to me. We entered the session on the basis of negotiation, but in fact there was little to discuss. What was available was a place for three in the most ambitious project ever to take place on this planet. The three scientists had their expertise in an unusual field to offer. The three men had formed their own ideas of what to expect, based on current gossip in the scientific world; now they were presented with factual details. Now they were asked to make an unequivocal decision! Curt and Paul were eager to start. The excitement created by my calm and deliberately casual replies to their animated questions seemed to arouse their imagination and stimulate fantastic notions; they were almost dancing with excitement and shouted crazy fanciful thoughts to each other. Herman, however, did not join in with the wild suppositions and statements flying about; he was the one to ask sceptical questions about finance and large-scale facilities and persistently about the location of the project.

"Where on earth can you carry out an operation such as you are describing in secret?" he insisted on asking.

Of course I was relieved to find that at least some of the important details of the scheme were apparently still secure. The two enthusiasts tried there hardest to change the gloomy attitude of their companion. He however merely became more obtuse, and obstructive to all argument to try to alter his outlook. This centred on the things that they would necessarily have to abandon—their boat, their home, their happy and comfortable lifestyle, all for the uncertainties of an unproved venture.

"Just imagine the risks," he argued, "and what, realistically, are the prospects of success?" Herman constantly poured cold water over the outcome of the enterprise. The argument between the three men became bitter and heated. I excused myself to join Jon on deck; here I explained what was happening below and my intention.

Eventually Curt appeared and in sad tones said, "I'm afraid we can't get Herman to agree with Paul and me. He was as enthusiastic as we were last night but he gets these moods; something we've said has probably upset him. He'll get over it in a day or two. We'll have to return to port now it's getting late."

I said, "Let me have a final word with you all." I led the way to the big stateroom and once there faced the three scientists, and in a firm determined voice stated flatly:

"We have not told you this before but now you must know. We are being watched and chased by some organisation that will stop at nothing to frustrate our plans; we were attacked in our hotel last night. We do not intend to return to our room and, what is more, we have no intention of allowing you to return home either." Ignoring the startled looks that appeared on the faces of the three men, I went on, "I've revealed far too much of our plans to risk allowing you any more contact with the world you are familiar with, so far as you are concerned the die is cast.

"Okay Jon." The gas projectors appeared instantly, and again three bodies slumped to the floor.

"Now to deal with Samson," I grunted. "Are you ready?"

Jon nodded, a grim smile on his face. I reflected on how reassuring this dark enigmatic Chinese appeared in a tight corner with the prospect of difficulties ahead. We made our way up to the bridge where the robot was confidently controlling the boat's progress through the water in the velvet darkness. I went to his side, thus blocking his rear vision.

"What do you make of that?" I asked pointing to a bright light on the port side. The robot immediately answered, "That's a warning light on the main TV antenna on the outskirts of Lausanne, Chung Peng." At this instant Jon, who silent as a shadow had made his way behind the robot, dropped a noose of mooring line over the head and shoulders and finally over those lethally strong arms. He drew the noose tight and made it fast.

The robot offered no resistance.

I cautiously told the robot to turn to face me, and then looking straight into his eyes said, "I want you to lie down on the floor and remain there until I speak to you again." Although I knew it to be impossible, I felt sure I saw an expression of puzzlement cross the robot's face as he followed the instructions. Once down, Jon quickly lashed a further rope around the legs and again an extra coil around the arms. "That should hold him," he grinned. We both were sweating slightly. We had anticipated a struggle. "Well, that was easy enough, what's next?"

"Get away from here as fast as we can," I said. "Everything is too quiet for my peace of mind."

My nautical experience proved useful in mastering the unfamiliar controls. We set a course, which took us due south. Jon and I were urgently in need of a plan of action in not much more than twenty-four hours. We had incapacitated five men who had tried to waylay us, kidnapped three Swiss citizens, and were now stealing a boat that was the property of the three scientists. That would cause some fur to fly, not least because the police must be involved by now. Now we had to get three men and a robot from a lake into the centre of Switzerland, to a remote region in China. "An interesting prospect," I mused thoughtfully.

"I'm glad it's not my problem," thought Jon.

After some discussion we decided that the simplest method of hiding the bodies would be to keep them on the boat; that meant transporting the cruiser by road to the nearest open water.

"The nearest point in the Med. is Cannes," I stated. "It's approximately 350 km, that's unless you have a better idea?"

Jon made no comment. He was wondering how on earth one could move a boat as big as this by road anyway? Cannes or anywhere else seemed of little consequence to him. Fortunately I did know what I was talking about, so after consulting the lake map and then checking the navigation beacons, I set course for Ferney. To avoid attracting attention we kept the boat's speed to a prudent level compatible with night-time navigation, although our instincts were to race away as fast as possible. I remained at the boat controls all night whilst Jon spent a considerable period of his time concocting a coded report for transmission to base as soon as the opportunity presented itself. We had been out of contact with any form of assistance from the time that we had left the airport on our arrival in Switzerland. Now it was urgent to organise additional help; it was obvious that we were going to need it.

Ferney marina, despite the early hour of our arrival, was bustling with activity as we made our way slowly to the slip. Curt had joined us on the bridge and was directing operations. When Curt came round from his initial unconsciousness as the effect of the gas wore off, I offered him a choice: "You can help with the inevitable or join Herman and Paul." They had each been given an anaesthetic injection. Happily for me, when given the chance—"Help us to do what you are in favour of anyway, or go to sleep for another twenty-four hours"—he chose to help. Curt knew where the best transport facilities were to be found and despite the demand for immediate attention, as we lubricated every hand with generous helpings of monetary oil we made the necessary arrangements in short order.

While all this was being done Jon had made a video call to the Chinese Embassy in Geneva. With the display of his security clearance he spoke to no less a person than the Ambassador himself! The Ambassador's ruffled appearance suggested that he had been aroused from his slumbers very recently. It was Jon's first experience of the prestige his clearance had on diplomatic staff and he was suitably impressed. He passed on the coded message for urgent transmission; he had to smile at the stir caused by the destination he gave, which was none other than the Imperial Palace.

When Jon returned to the quayside two hours later he was greeted by Curt saying, "It was quite easy really, we had the boat hauled down to Cannes last year with the same people, so this is just like a re-run."

Jon was amazed at how massive the cruiser looked when it was out of the water, how very much higher it appeared than he had expected. "I see that you have the plasticol cover on; well, that might help a bit—at least the name is hidden." I elected to remain inside the boat. "I can catch up with some sleep and be on hand in case of problems with Herman and

Paul." Jon and Curt went into the cab with the two professional drivers of the large transporter.

Once we moved off Jon was filled with admiration for the splendour of the mountain scenery through which we passed. The sunshine caused the snowy peaks to sparkle with ice patches acting like prisms to reflect the brightness into rainbow colours, which gave the mountain a magical aura. On the mountain's lower slopes the traditional Swiss houses looked like models from a child's storybook; scattered around were black and white cows cropping contentedly at the lush green pasture, all of which added to this dream-like picture. These images however were lost all too soon as the roadway entered the first of many tunnels cut arrow straight through the granite mountains. Ten hours of steady driving later we were in Cannes and within a short time found ourselves refloated in the warm waters of the Mediterranean. Curt, with Jon in attendance, dealt with the harbour formalities, while I checked water, fuel and provisions on the cruiser. We had cast off and were making a slow departure when a large uniformed figure raced along the quay and leaped aboard. "Stop!" he cried. "I've a report from Lausanne that I want some answers to." I was on the bridge controlling the boat's passage and glanced quickly at Jon, but said nothing. The big policeman repeated, "Stop at once."

He was a giant of a man weighing more than two hundred pounds and confident of giving commands which others obeyed; he had climbed the ladder to the control cockpit. When I ignored his order, his face took on an unpleasant grin. "So you need a little persuasion, do you?" Drawing his electric baton he was about to give me a jab when robot Paul appeared with Curt close behind. The big policeman, seeing the way in which Paul was advancing directly towards him, hastily transferred his attack to the robot. The first blow had no effect whatever, so he quickly adjusted the charge control to maximum. Normally an almost lethal shock would have been delivered to the unfortunate victim. The charge crackled on the robot's chest but had no other effect; the robot then went on to grab the policeman by his uniform jacket, lifted him up bodily from the deck of the cockpit like a toy doll and tossed him into the sea. He made a terrific splash, then spluttering, shouting and angrily waving his massive fists, he swore passionate vengeance on the boat's occupants, his cries gradually becoming fainter as we drew away.

"Now the fat will be in the fire," I said, voicing all our thoughts. "We'd better run for it!" Once we were clear of the harbour I turned to Curt and said, "Well, I think that we can safely say that you have demonstrated your loyalty with that show. You could obviously just as easily turned the robot onto us had you wanted to." Curt merely smiled and said, "There was no need to restrain our robot so I set him loose, and just in time it seems. Now if you'll allow me, I'll show you what this little beauty can really do."

I stepped aside to allow Curt to take my place. Curt immediately pulled a lever marked Rotors. On each side or the cruiser, what appeared to be porthole covers slowly unfolded; there were five on each side and when fully extended formed a platform along each side of the boat from bow to stern; with a flap on each side to form a skirt, the cruiser seemed to be twice as wide. When this operation was completed, the operator pressed a button. A roar like thunder burst over us, the boat rocked a little, then heaved itself clear out of the water.

"And now let's go!" yelled Curt as he pulled the throttle back and the boat fairly leapt forward to race across the calm sea.

When the surprise and excitement had died down a little, Curt, shouting to make his voice heard, yelled, "Now you'll realise why we came here last year. The lake isn't big enough to run this beauty in."

Now that the police had joined the hunt in addition to our unknown enemies, Jon and I had more problems to exercise our brains with, not least of which was, what course to set? After some discussion we headed west towards Majorca. We continued at high speed tearing through the wind and spray, constantly buffeted despite the calm sea, knowing that we would attract attention on radar screens. But as night fell we were close to the Balearics. Curt cut the acceleration and returned the rotors to their housing, thus resuming the shape and profile of a normal cruiser. We then reversed the direction in which we had been charging along and headed southeast.

At exactly 21.05hrs, Jon connected a personal coding device to the cruiser's transmitter to send a high-speed location signal; the transmission lasted only 15 seconds. "Long enough if it's expected," grunted Jon. He was right; three hours later he received the reply that he was waiting for. "We'll be picked up at dawn!" Jon asked Curt for details of the craft's displacement and dimensions which he included in his next message at 03.05.

Dawn was at 06.24 that day; at 06.05 Jon was waiting anxiously by the ship radio. The message when it came was in code; it was a tense period before he could eventually report to Curt and me. "They want us to make maximum speed. Are you sure we can make fifty knots?"

"Easily," came the reply.

"Well, let's do it! They say they will pick us up in ten minutes but fifty knots is essential."

Soon the cruiser was racing along over the deep blue sea on its cushion of air. No one had any idea what was going to happen; we couldn't speak above the roar of the motors running flat out, so we just hung on and looked around in the thin pale light of morning. Suddenly a giant shadow loomed from behind us; it grew bigger and came closer, then a few metres above exactly matched our course and speed. Then the shadow surged ahead, upwards and banking away, we were then able to make out the shape of a gigantic aircraft. The plane made a wide circle before approaching again from the rear almost touching the sea. "What on earth are they playing at?" demanded Curt. "They're going to ram us!" He was speaking to himself, for no one could hear anything above the roar of the cruiser's engines, and on top of that the overwhelming noise from the aircraft's eight rotors. This time as the plane approached closer, an opening appeared in the lower portion of the fuselage. The massive plane was skimming the top of the waters; it came closer, closer and closer, then in seconds it engulfed the cruiser: our boat was inside the giant belly of the aircraft!

I quickly summed up the situation and slammed the throttle control shut, and then Curt, dazed and bemused, shut down the air cushion rotors.

Now less than one minute later the front doors of the plane were closing. Through the narrowing aperture I could see the dark waters of the Med dropping away beneath...

"Well, that was the most exciting experience of my life," laughed a marvelling Curt; Jon and I exchanged relieved grins with each other. In our wildest dreams we could never have imagined being picked up!... Meaning exactly that!

We all stared round the cavernous interior of this plane, then turned to look at the pilot who had performed this minor miracle of snatching a boat from the sea as he introduced himself five minutes later. "I wouldn't like to guess at his age," I thought.

The pilot had a jaunty manner. He wore a multi-coloured silk scarf around his neck but nevertheless the creases radiating from his eyes and prematurely grey hair gave him a distinctive appearance, which belied his nonchalant attitude. "The last time we did this," he laughed, "was to pick up water from a lake two miles long and three metres deep during the great forest fires in Sansu province three years ago. I need a little practice occasionally." He refused outright to discuss his unique aircraft; then after saying that he had orders to deliver us to a point just short of Hainan, he left us to pass the next six hours as best we may.

When the plane came down again the bow doors slowly opened and the waters of the China Sea flooded in. The sea level rose till our boat floated easy, and we slowly made our way forward and out of the hold; as we drew away from the massive plane we saw the doors close and then the eight engines started to rotate the eight giant airscrews.

I could just see the Island of Hainan looming out of the haze to the north and as we headed towards home we heard the roar of the extraordinary aircraft take off behind us.

And so a few hours later, after saying goodbye to Jon Chan and wishing him well, I introduced three slightly bewildered Swiss scientists to my wife and Ched Taylor.

CHAPTER THIRTEEN

---◆---

The following day, after a long deep sleep and a satisfying reunion with Beth, I had a detailed discussion with Ched before entering the private jet, which was to take me north. I agreed with Ched's view that it was necessary for one of us to remain at H.Q. "The three girls can look after the screening of new volunteers," Ched said, "but there's still a hell of a backlog of materials to order, and now we are getting requests for really advanced equipment and instrumentation; some of the stuff is not even in commercial production." Both Ched and I accepted that to get laboratories to part with some of the information which the venture desired for our purposes might mean disclosing Ched's identity to enable us to take advantage of his international reputation. This disclosure together with the destination would attract attention and speculation towards China.

"Well, we've not done too badly up to now," I mused, "but I think it prudent to close shop here on Hainan as soon as possible; let's say six weeks at the outside. This place will become too exposed for any of our party to stay longer."

My flight was to Suchow, a town near to the end of the Great Wall of China. Here I transferred to a military helicopter for the next stage of the journey to Pegasus. The helicopter put me down at a military base seventy kilometres away, so the last section of his journey was to be made by jeep. I took a keen interest in the security involved before being allowed to take my place in the jeep. I could not but wonder at how quickly we had been spotted in Switzerland.

First I was seated in front of a videophone while the military police contacted Hainan H.Q., who confirmed that Ro Stern had left there that morning and that the image they were seeing was indeed that of Roland Stern; in addition they confirmed that the documents were in order. When at last I was seated in the open truck I met for the first time the person who was to play such a major role in all our futures. I laughingly remarked about the time taken to establish my identity. Hank, who was to be my driver, smiled briefly in reply, then said, "You've not finished yet; wait until we get to Pegasus. Even this journey is logged and I have a one-trip permit which is timed to the minute." I said, "Where do you fit into this set-up?" Hank, in his standard unassuming manner and with a slight smile, replied, "I suppose that really I'm Mac's errand boy."

I was taken aback at this "errand boy"—it seemed an odd answer; to my personal knowledge all the recruits I had met or spoken to had at least one degree in some field or other and often several. Then the name Mac registered; that must be MacGreggor, the structural engineer and site manager. I remembered the demand for 500,000 tent pegs and towels. My eyes narrowed slightly. I intended to find out exactly what had happened to those pegs. I had already considered the consequences likely to result from sloppy attitudes and associated indiscipline. I also had decided views on the requirements needed to keep this project under control and to maintain an over-riding sense of purpose in everyone's mind. The thought of any sort of passenger such as an errand boy put my back up.

It was a pity the two of us started our association on such a mistaken basis, for Hank was the best person on the base to supply the information that I most needed; but many sound relationships have a rocky foundation.

We arrived to a hive of activity with people rushing in all directions to transfer supplies from storage area to building site; long trains of concrete sections towed by roaring tractors sounding their horns to warn people to give way threw up clouds of sand. There was dust and noise everywhere. The tent village had originally been arranged in some semblance of order, but where the tents had been torn or damaged and subsequently abandoned, they were now flapping untidily. There were oil drums scattered about and the debris that accumulates where groups of people gather without positive direction. Apparently there was no interest in maintaining their surroundings in an orderly manner; black plastic bags were scattered everywhere, and the overall impression was one of neglect and lack of interest. I was appalled at the sight and wondered what morale was like. There was little time to ponder; Hank delivered me to one of the few orderly structures in evidence. These were large semi-circular affairs, constructions formed from vast polygons of yellow plastic material and as I was to discover, maintained their shape by means of a slightly increased internal air pressure. Several of these structures were clearly for military use. Later I was to find that one housed the temporary hydroponic tanks, but for now all my attention was directed to my present destination which was clearly marked, "New Arrivals". A big red bearded, hard eyed, craggy faced man who introduced himself as "Pete Morgan, head of base security," met me at the entrance.

I held out my hand. "From the procedures I've already seen, I expect you know that I'm Roland Stern." Pete nodded. "We were told you were on your way this morning. Now, I know that you are nominally head of this enterprise, but I suggest that you go through our routine new entry procedure; we need to have your vital life signs on our computer for regular health checking and in case of accidents. We also need to check your identity against our records to authorise the issue of your personal security certificate."

I thought, "At least this section sounds efficient."

My opinion was amply reinforced a full hour later after a session in the interrogation chair where my heart rate was checked, my blood pressure monitored, my perspiration analysed and my retina pattern confirmed—all the time being expected to answer searching questions about my previous occupation, college grades, and names of parents, brothers, sisters and places of residence. Finally I was given my security pass—a tough sealed "Plasterlite" badge that adhered firmly to my lapel with a "Lecto-stat" pad. I was also given a ring which was fitted carefully onto my finger containing the necessary code to deactivate the field when I wished to change clothes. I was warned never to attempt to move without this identification. The pass enclosed a three-dimensional likeness with my name clearly displayed and somewhere inside a personal security code. I felt as though I had been wrung out and squeezed dry when I finally emerged and had to smile wryly as Pete Morgan said earnestly, "I'd welcome any suggestions you could make to improve our procedures." I was then told that the next step for new entrants was the medical tent; my thoughts immediately flashed back to the last occasion I had been involved with the Doctor in charge here. It was a grim reminder that for all the checks on new personnel, some spy, possibly more than one, had probably managed to infiltrate this project. I wondered what had happened to the widows of the men made victims by this determined and aggressive effort to penetrate our defences.

I was given a thorough medical examination and finally passed through the irradiation booth. I was then shown to my tented accommodation. I quickly realised the need for a good general manager and wished that Ched were here to get things organised. My next move was to have a detailed look around to try to find a datum point from which to start working. Some time later after making enquiries around the base, I was led to ask for Hank.

Hank arrived as I was about to leave the tent designated "Site Office". Although I was far from happy with the undisciplined air and appearance of the base, I was careful not to comment on this. I intended to keep an open mind until I had seen all that there was to see. For his part, Hank was unusually subdued with this grim unsmiling Roland Stern, who he now knew to be one of the original founders of this enterprise. He wondered if now he would find out what it was all for. All new arrivals had had secrecy drummed into them and as most were strangers to one another they only ever discussed their day-to-day affairs when they gathered socially. Hank was popular but no one had gone so far as to discuss with him the ultimate objective of all this activity. At my request Hank took me over the entire site. I soon realised the soundness of the advice that Hank would be best for this job; he was on friendly terms with all we met, and I determined to keep him by my side until I became more familiar with the hundreds of strange faces we encountered.

When we caught up with MacGreggor I said, "Could we have a quiet word together?"

Mac, who a moment before had been desperately trying to convince a young man with a full beard and large black rimmed spectacles that in spite of the fact that he could calculate the exact point of balance, it was dangerous to leave a concrete slab in such a position while he erected an upright. Mac nodded and said, "Of course, I'm sorry, I was nae at reception to meet ye Mr Stern, but with so much unskilled labour about, all keen to get on with the job, I have nightmares about the risks we're taking. I'm amazed that we've had nae one kilt."

Daylight was failing and as this set the end to the working day, Mac and I returned to the mess tent. Here we found a table in a quiet corner and Mac proceeded to bring me up to date with progress. After some general observations he concluded, "We have the first floor structure completed and are well on with the second level now. This means that the ground floor workshop area is ready for fitting out. Ben Hoyt and Si Lucas have a team with them working on that; I expect the second floor to be completed in three days; that's the up-to-date position. I suppose that ye'll know the rest from the weekly reports." I noted a faintly sarcastic tone. "Now, can I ask ye something?"

"Certainly," I replied.

Mac took a deep breath, his Scots accent becoming ever stronger. "Are ye here to run this set up?" Without waiting for a reply, in an exasperated voice, he cried, "I've been engaged to build the queerest structure on earth under the most ridiculous conditions. I've been given nae budget, I git whativer I ask for but until recently I was expected to do it with completely unskilled labour. I cain't get answers to most of ma questions and if we venture far oot inta t'desert we have a yallow soojer sticking a stun stick into oowr face." His cheeks were flushed and his eyes bright with passion as he waited for a reply.

"You'll feel better for getting that lot off your chest." I smiled for the first time since my arrival. "As for my authority, I have been elected provisional leader of Project Pegasus. But I'm afraid I'm not prepared to answer any more of your legitimate queries until we have a totally secure base. So all that I can tell you immediately is that the sooner we have the building completed, the sooner you'll get your answers." And with that response, an angry Mac had to be satisfied.

I then looked around the now full mess tent. I saw Oval talking to Teng Ho. They were sitting with the rest of the founder members and were only minus the three girls and Ched, who were still in Hainan. I excused myself and went across to join the few faces I was familiar with. As I moved across the dining area I was conscious of the many curious glances I received from the assembled company; the word had obviously gone round that the boss had arrived.

When initial greetings were over, I started on the problem uppermost in my mind. "The last thing I want is a private office; everyone here is in this thing up to their ears, but until we have guaranteed security from outside interference I'm reluctant to include the whole 'jam bang' in our immediate discussions." The rest of the party accepted these sentiments and began talking of individual problems. It was soon apparent that many projects were impossible until the permanent building was ready for occupation. There was one exception, however.

Oval reminded us that the Death Ray required more development. "I have met a fellow Physicist who I could work with. Ideally we need two or three others, preferably in electronics and possibly one in data processing," she concluded.

I agreed to put this subject at the head of my programme.

The following day I made another tour of the site, greeting as many people as possible, trying to remember faces and qualifications. I was asking Ben Hoyt, who I knew slightly, how his lab was progressing. "Pretty well, now we have a power supply; we don't need much in the way of specials you know." Ben spoke with enthusiasm. "We concluded the calculations at Caltec. We can start on our first production model now. We plan to build several, increasing the diameter of the giro each time, but once we exceed one metre, we shall need a test pit well away from anyone and anything." I nodded. "I'll see what's available," I promised.

I went quickly to a meeting with Oval and Mac. I performed the introductions and said, "If you would explain your ideal requirements, Dr Himnal, and let's see how near we can come to meeting them." I smiled meaningfully at Mac.

"We don't need much space; but we must have thick concrete to shield the rest of the community," stated Oval emphatically.

"That's nae problem," replied Mac. "Concrete we have in plenty, just tell me what ye need."

That's a promising start, I thought, leaving the two very different figures discussing dimensions; the tall blonde young woman, athletic and bronzed, but exhibiting a tired appearance with dark stains around her fine blue eyes; and the short and wiry grey headed Scot who looked older than his forty-three years and whose face, for once, had lost its perpetual frown.

The following weeks developed into some sort of routine for me. Each morning I would set off to make a round of the site, and each day something prevented me completing it; increasingly I had to reassure disaffected venturers that this building work was an essential part of our ultimate plans. Unfortunately for the others, I would not disclose the full story, and so was reduced to platitudes and encouragement to help finish the current job on hand.

Then the great storm struck, battering the whole of the tented accommodation flat. It lasted for two dreary days. No hot food or water was available and sleeping was restricted to wherever there was some sort of shelter in the still unfinished building. The storm reduced spirits to an all-time low. This placed a great burden on my stamina and purpose and even greater stress on my patience in dealing with petty quibbles and squabbling in the community. Even Hank, that normally sunny character who always had a silly grin on his silly face, according to one of his detractors, fell to complaining to Annette. She had become his regular table companion these days; he grumbled of how he had forgotten what a good steak tasted like; he hadn't had a decent meal since he'd arrived at this dump. Annette made no reply. She could have told him that there was no animal protein in the camp; all protein in whatever form it appeared was derived from vegetable sources.

So she said nothing and next day Hank was over his sulks. The final design for the building called for a deep ditch to surround the gigantic beehive-shaped structure. I was watching the retractable roadway that was to be the only entrance to Pegasus undergoing load testing when Hank came to inform me of a top priority notification of an incoming video call in ten minutes. When the call was transmitted it was from Ched in Hainan; he was in high spirits. "I've decided that we can shut up shop here," he announced. It was just four weeks after our last conference. "The girls have passed the last applicant through and I can work through the Chinese central buying organisation for anything else that we may need. We'll be up in three days!"

I sighed with relief. I looked forward to Ched's experience to organise the multitude of differing professionals here into some sort of order. I could easily deal with strategy, but day-to-day details bored me. The interior of the dome had reached level four now—the first of the personnel accommodation levels. As a result the fitting out of level five could begin; this floor was to be a recreational area. There was to be a well equipped kitchen and a comfortable dining room; there would be a gymnasium and sporting facilities. There were also plans to create an auditorium large enough to seat the entire company, fitted with the latest entertainment wonder, larger than life, but otherwise indistinguishable from living people—three dimensional video-scope.

Well, there was some good news to discuss at table that evening. I was cheered at the prospect of having Beth by my side once more. We had been parted previously, and since we were married often for weeks at a time, but I was feeling particularly lonely of late. "I must be getting old," I told myself.

Teng Ho Pot was in a jubilant mood as he proceeded to explain, much to the amusement of his companions, how the ancient Chinese race had had to show these jumped up Americans how to throw a plate! He was referring to the dilemma that Ben's team had found themselves in as they tried to increase the diameter of their gyroscopes to more than .5m. Over this size, the flywheel disintegrated as the peripheral speed exceeded 10,000km.

Teng Ho had shrewdly suggested they use a ceramic base laced with iron particles for the magnetic properties required. It was to be reinforced with carbon fibres, then thrown into shape on a revolving disk. "Just like my great, great, great, grandparent used to make plates and saucers," laughed Teng Ho.

The following days I was concentrating attention on the layout of the reception area. Happily I had Pete Morgan here to direct the security that was so vital. "Fort Knox will have nothing on this place," grunted a hard-faced Pete. I was thinking, "If Oval's enterprise succeeds we won't need security screens or drawbridges as long as we stay inside our Beehive."

Ched with his wife Eva, Beth and Lin ho, arrived as the first dormitory block was ready for occupation, so they at least were spared the restrictions of tented accommodation.

They had entered Pegasus through the newly completed reception area where the newcomers had all to pass through the standard entry security system. I was smiling as I awaited their emergence. As each individual appeared from the interrogation they were shown to a comfortable seat and offered a mild stimulating drink. Without exception they let out a massive sigh and collapsed into the deep seats.

"I thought we were pretty shrewd and forthright on Hainan," stated a subdued Eva, "but I never expected to feel so positively drained after an interview that's only supposed to establish my identity."

I said, "You'll be asked if you have any suggestions to improve it before long."

We were heading for our private living quarters. The floor covering was soft and springy underfoot, a carpet with a mottled pattern of brown and beige. The walls were covered in a resilient fabric in large geometric patterns in colours of red, gold and green, which stood out vividly against the beige background. Illumination came from hundreds of tiny glowing bulbs stuck to the ceiling. Beth asked about these.

"One of our own inventions, actually conceived, tested and produced on the premises. A by-product from the 'Lite-Agg' experiments; while we were waiting to get the correct volume to the silica aggregate, one of the electronics people casually mentioned the similarity between the scrap product and lighting bulbs. As there was plenty of waiting time, inactive and underused brains that had nothing better than concrete to think about, started to throw ideas around and these are the result.

"The whole ceiling is covered in a soft mortar on top of a conducting matrix; then these miniature light bulbs are blown on. The circuit is charged with a background voltage to give the dim illumination, but this is increased by the static electricity which is produced as we pass. You'll notice how the ceiling brightens as we approach and fades as we move away."

Beth asked, "What material have you used to decorate the wall? From what you told me about the vast quantities of concrete you used, I had visions of living in a huge building with nothing but grey walls to look at."

"It's certainly a concrete structure, but all living and

recreational areas are sprayed with this synthetic material; there are two bases that we are experimenting with at present.

"The first is protein which we are growing in the Hydroponic tanks—it's really a modification of Soya. It's slightly different to the strain we use for foodstuffs and we can bring it to maturity in twenty-one days. Then the other also comes from the tanks, but in this case we use the leaves as a source of cellulose, which gives us a softer rayon type fibre. One of our chemists, a giant black called Buz Obas, spends his time with a small party digging up different types of shale and clays, roasting and grinding them and has already produced the three primary colour pigments this enables us to colour the fibres to most shades. So we are adding a little sophistication to our concrete.

CHAPTER FOURTEEN

The following three months passed quickly enough for everyone who was to become a permanent resident of Pegasus. The exceptions were those few traitors who were more interested in scuttling the venture; but in such a manner as to be free to enjoy the rewards, which they had been promised.

In late December, as we were rising from a substantial breakfast, I commented to Ched, "Now that the exterior work is completed and we've cleaned away the building rubbish, I feel that it's time we started living in accordance with our proposals for the future. However, before we can do that, which means cutting ourselves off from the outside altogether, we must hold a general conference to announce that Stage One of our plans is now completed and make a statement to re-affirm our objectives."

Ched nodded in agreement. "But first we'd better call a meeting of the founders, to hear their views."

Consequently at dinner that same evening the original band of thirteen people, the initiators of what was to be "the event of the century," sat together again for our final meeting. It was hard for us to realise how far we had succeeded with what had started almost as a holiday gag; there was nothing new to discuss, for the programme to be announced at the conference had been agreed upon long ago. "It is just to allow you all to approve of the timing that we're here," I said, "and I suggest that the time is now."

Ched chipped in, "Well, the anti-grav exhibit is ready for demonstrating!"

Some time later, as conversation was becoming nostalgic and memories which referred to our first meeting so long ago began to dominate the discussion, we agreed to call a general meeting for tomorrow. The following day the announcement of a General Conference for that evening was made. The base immediately took on an air of excitement and speculation; this affected people in many differing ways.

Some decided that events were progressing at last and were anxious to get started, while others became depressed.

Hank, gushing with eagerness, said to Mac, "Well, at last we're going to be told what all this is for."

"Aye," replied a sombre Mac, "I wonder if ye'll be so chirpy tomorrow when you realise what I've let ye in for?" Mac had a premonition that the news when it came would have fateful consequences. However, an insouciant Hank bubbled on.

"I wouldn't be surprised if they weren't going to build a giant rocket to fly to Mars or perhaps Venus! What else can all these professors and scientists be doing here?"

This comment did nothing to cheer Mac's gloomy thoughts; he'd already had the same idea, but he knew more of the world than Hank did. He was one of the silent observers who realised that odd facts had a way of disappearing from the news. In these days when it seemed impossible to keep a secret about anything, there was never any shortage of information about corruption in government, or scandal concerning personalities' "affairs". Even a clandestine film of five well known entertainers, relaxing in a communal sex frolic, had been shown on international television. But Mac knew that space flight was a taboo subject and he felt sure that whatever else it might be, this was not a rocket launching base. Yet in spite of his doubts he had overheard many remarks that he could associate with nothing else but space and then more recently, once the frenzied activity of the building work had eased and he had time to look around and reflect, he had puzzled over what on earth all this activity could possibly be for? And then the tremendous effort that went into security here. Mac was one of the first to discover that security was just as tight to restrict departure as it was on entry. He was indifferent regarding his own future; he had no close family or friends to consider but was passionately concerned about Hank who was here at Mac's personal invitation.

"I'm responsible for him," thought Mac, "a young life which I have no moral right to interfere with."

Beth was also apprehensive. She was aware of the excitement in the air and wondered "if any of the candidates will wish to drop-out when the inevitability of forthcoming events were fully restated". I nodded thoughtfully. "It's certainly a possibility, but we can contain any personal problems. What disturbs me is that there's been no further indication of outside interference; nothing has gone wrong since that explosion business—we've suffered nothing more! I don't like waiting for something to happen when I don't know what form it may take."

Meanwhile in the assembly hall Ben and Si had their own problems. "I'm glad we had these end walls fitted," said Ben.

"I had a hell of a job getting Mac to add them at such short notice and I don't think for one minute he believed my story of improving the acoustics; but at least when we go up tonight, if I don't calculate exactly were to hold the rev's they'll take the bump and not our heads." Si grinned, adding mischievously, "Always supposing we don't go up through the roof altogether and perhaps land on the moon!"

They were putting the final touches to their demonstration "anti-grav" device. This was in fact the platform or stage in the assembly hall which now had a reinforced concrete wall built on at each end. A long curved table occupied the stage with a rich ruby-coloured drape along the front edge, which contrasted nicely with the light grey carpet of the stage floor. There were thirteen seats arranged behind the table and Ben was busy setting up his control equipment at one end.

"We'd better arrange for security to keep the doors locked until we come back; we don't want some inquisitive amateur organist trying to make music on this little box of tricks."

This was a sly dig at Eva, Ched's wife, who had been making great efforts to encourage all the venturers to take up some musical instrument for their future entertainment.

The long day gradually came to an end; the evening meal was a raucous affair, everyone realising that a crossroad had been reached and although all had been recruited to fly to the stars, very few had any idea how this was to be achieved. They were also conscious that there would be no return, so excitement and anticipation filled every heart. There were as many differing expectations and hopes as there were minds to conjure up images. For many, the sheer adventure was sufficient. For others the fascination of seeing more of the universe personally instead of being restricted to unresolved theories proved an irresistible attraction. Against this satisfaction had to be set the regret of not being able to say, "I told you so," to that idiot in Milan University. Then there was the prospect of creating a new style of living; a setting without the faults and problems of this world. A world without the extremes of rich and poor; a society of equality where all were of equal importance and value, a world of social justice. I was among the latter, but in my heart of hearts I wondered if such idealism was attainable.

The clamour intensified; spirits became exhilarated, the atmosphere charged with excitement and eagerness to hear what was to happen. Eventually the meal came to an end and there was a general move towards the assembly hall. Ben made sure that he was the first person inside and made his way to his seat on the platform. Hank as usual was sitting with Annette. "I'm dying to know what this is all about," he said.

Annette smiled. "I suppose that I'll be able to talk more freely after tonight," she said. "It's very difficult having to wonder all the time if I'm telling you something I'm not supposed to." Hank replied, "You've done pretty well up to now. I'm also curious to know what part you play." His eyes travelled up her slender arms to a gently curving neck and beautiful face. "You don't look a bit like a scientist to me, you're far too pretty." Annette smiled again. He was always paying her compliments about her looks and slim figure; she allowed herself to dream of the future and wondered if Hank would be going with them.

He knew nothing of the project or the future that the colonists were contemplating. She felt ashamed of herself for fantasising about a future with Hank when Pierre's death was so recent. But she was honest enough to accept that she thought of Hank and the prospect of living together more often than she remembered her life with Pierre. Beth would be able to explain, had she been asked, that Annette was merely displaying symptoms common to orphans who had an overwhelming need to be wanted, to belong.

When every person in the building had arrived and found seats, Ro Stern, who was in the centre of the platform, stood and called for order.

I had no need to repeat this request. Silence was immediately accorded, and expectation was intense. I was wearing a miniature transmitting microphone on my collar, which clearly relayed my rather quiet voice to the public address system and thence to every corner of the hall.

I began to speak.

"I have been selected by the founders of this enterprise who are seated at this table, to lead you to a star system which is 125 years distance from here! When we reach the system we have to search for a suitable place on which to land and establish a new home. The reason for constructing our present building here is to give us all experience, to enable us to repeat this if necessary when we find a planet, in case of unfavourable atmospheric conditions.

"Many of you may not realise that we are already living on our own grown and processed food, which again is in preparation for our future needs. We intend to establish an ethical society of limited private ownership and minimum rules. There will to be no weapons of any sort! If we meet something we don't like we will solve the problem by applied brain power, not fire power. That is one of this world's mistakes, which we will not repeat. From this minute there will be no communication with any person outside the building. You will be able to leave farewell messages if you wish for delivery after our departure.

"You have all been selected as being able and willing to contribute to this venture. We now enjoy a completely closed environment; we will produce our own atmosphere, grow our own food, make our own dress and entertainment. There will no longer be any need to restrict our conversation or discussion of our work with any other person present; we are all in this together.

"Now I wish to introduce the various primary group spokesmen or women; I repeat, spokesmen or women—there is to be no individual ruler. My present position will terminate immediately when we have established our new home."

Although I had proposed the idea of a dictatorship to keep the entire scheme on a tightly concentrated course, I was very conscious of the risk which such power could bring. The drug of absolute power has wrecked many lives and societies throughout history and we had placed the strictest limits on the time that it should be available for use in our future!

I continued: "Each principle category of expertise will select one person to represent them in council, which will make all future decisions.

"Right, I first wish to introduce our Chemists, who are represented by Dr Buz Obas." The giant black man stood up, looked around with a wide grin on his face and resumed his seat again.

"Professor Teng Ho Pot as well as being the son-in-law of the President of China without whose support we could not have started this enterprise, is an outstanding metallurgist.

"From Physics we have Dr Oval Himnal.

"Keeping us all fed, we have our representative botanist, Professor Annette Lefarge." I continued with several more categories of learning and then said, "We are fortunate to have with us three men who are leaders from the world of robotics. We will benefit greatly from the help of advanced androids which are largely the result of unprecedented achievements made recently by our three Swiss cybernetic engineers." I thought, I hope I haven't laid it on too thick, but I had learned that the three scientists responded to personal praise.

I went on: "I'm sure you will all remember Pete Morgan from your arrival here; your interrogation and security clearance!"

I paused to allow an outbreak of ribaldry to die down.

"We also have a strong medical, psychiatric, and stress therapeutic team here to keep us all sane and healthy. Take a bow, Dr Stronberg."

When all categories had been introduced, I continued, "Now finally I must tell you the founder members of 'Project Pegasus', after very careful consideration, have decided that notwith-standing our ultimate objective of forming an egalitarian society, have accepted that progress towards such an ambitious undertaking will demand strict discipline and single-mindedness:

"This will leave no room for debate!"

As I continued, my voice took on a grave and sombre tone: "To achieve our ambition will require dedication and continuing endeavour by everyone. To ensure that we reach this objective, and until our new colony is established, I have been offered and have accepted, dictatorial power.

"I am the final authority"

I paused. I fully intended these last words to register in the hushed assembly.

Then I nodded to Ben.

I remained standing. Ben thought, "I hope I can justify his confidence." He concentrated on his control panel.

The audience had hitherto ignored the faint hum that only now, as the note changed slightly, attracted attention.

Then there were gasps of astonishment and cries of concern as the concrete platform with tables and chairs, thirteen men and women and sizable concrete end walls, rose slowly and majestically into the roof space of the auditorium!

It was too much for the audience nearest to the platform. There was a scramble away towards the rear of the hall; there they turned to see the platform hovering perfectly steadily four metres above the floor.

Ben was laughing with relief. "We've done it, we've done it!" he yelled to Si.

I came to the front of the platform, held up my arms to quieten the noise of excited comments, and said, "Now you see demonstrated the method by which we will leave Earth.

"I throw the meeting open to questions."

After declaring the conference open for questions, I returned to my seat and asked Ched to take the chair.

Ben, with a delighted expression on his face, slowly returned the platform to its former position. "Anyone would think he didn't expect it to work," I laughed as I sat down next to Beth. She squeezed my hand and whispered, "It looks as though we're on our way at last!"

The first question was, "How does the anti-grav device work?"

Ben was still smiling; he started to explain the surprising

effects they had discovered once the velocity of iron approached the speed of light and in complete accordance with Einstein's theory demonstrating how velocity increased mass. "With mass increased, the nuclear structure of materials take on different magnetic properties, magnetism and gravity being manifestations of the same ultimate cosmic force; with velocity incorporated into the equation we developed a means of changing gravity: and by inference creating negative or, anti-gravity. Then by varying the velocity we could produce negative or non-gravity at will."

Hank, who had been holding Annette's hand until she stood up to acknowledge her introduction and heard her addressed as Professor, whispered, "Let's get out of this—I can't understand a word that's being said here and I want to talk to you." Once outside the assembly hall Hank went on, "What did he mean when he said that you were responsible for feeding us?"

Looking shrewdly into Hank's troubled face, Annette said, "I'll show you if you wish"—and she led the way to the elevators. Inside she fingered the indicator for the top level; she was amused to see how Hank stood away from her. "I'm still the same person, you know; just because you've heard of my title, it hasn't made me any different."

"It's made *me* feel different," said Hank dismally, "I'm nothing around here, I've no real job and no qualifications amongst all you professors, doctors and mathematicians and..."

"Don't be silly, everyone knows who you are and if anything goes wrong you're the first person they ask for to get things moving again." They had reached the top level now; although it was night and dark outside, this whole level was brightly illuminated. "This is where I work," said Annette.

The floor was laid out with row upon row of shallow ponds; these had been simply formed by arranging concrete beams into large rectangles. The beams were about thirty centimetres thick so that when one was placed on top of another and a sheet of Plastisol spread across and allowed to drape inside, then filled with water, a pond was easily made. Most of these ponds were filled with a dark-green large leafed plant; at intervals some of the ponds contained a brown coloured growth.

"Where does a botanist fit into growing giant water cress?" demanded a sulky Hank.

"My degree is in botany but I've spent most of my time recently studying the food that fish live on," explained Annette. "I then became involved in fish farming, then from growing high protein fish food I moved into developing aquaculture into a science that would allow people to eat and live far away from traditional methods of food production. It was this aspect of our work that attracted the recruiting team from this consortium. I'd no idea what we were letting ourselves into; Pierre rushed home one day, so excited, and said that we had this opportunity to work for an organisation that was to fly to the stars! He was so enthusiastic and I only ever wanted to please him. I didn't ask many questions; I didn't care, I only wanted to make Pierre happy, but it didn't last for long. Oh!" (Her voice broke) "How I've missed him." She stopped moving. Hank, who was following, carefully slipped his arms around her waist and squeezed gently. Annette was thinking of the last time she had been in bed with Pierre, back in the hotel on Hianan Island. She thought of how much she enjoyed Pierre's lovemaking; as she thought of that last night nearly a year ago, passion and desire flooded up through her. She was aware of a pounding in her breast, of her nipples becoming taut and hot. It took her seconds only to decide; she placed her hands over Hank's and slowly lifted them up to cover her full breasts.

She was panting with excitement now. Hank seemed at a loss to know what to do, so she bent forward a little and slowly waggled her bum against him, which had the desired effect; he turned her round and kissed her hard. He had to stoop to kiss Annette for he was over six foot and she only a little over five; so he sank to his knees and thrust his head into her bosom, his hands now snatching at the fastenings of her pale blue slacks. She tore at the buttons of her tunic and pulled it over her head; she wore nothing underneath so her proud firm breasts with the dark prominent nipples poked into his eye, then down his cheek and into his open lips. Her slacks were off now; she kicked them away and immediately reached to unfasten his. He was holding her so close that his pants wouldn't fall; she pulled her hands from the front and grabbed the waistband and pushed down. It was a struggle, a massive obstruction prevented them falling.   Now his hands were around the cheeks of her bottom, which felt like a large firm peach. His lips were soon kissing her flat belly. Gradually he heaved himself upright, taking Annette with him, and her legs were wrapped around his. His mind was in a whirl; he was unable to think coherently, so of course she had to lead; one hand around his neck to hold on, the other went down between them and carefully found and guided his baton-like member home to her eager pulsing valley of pleasure.   Three quick thrusts was all it took before he exploded; this was followed by a state of blissful wonder. "It's like all my dreams rolled into one," breathed Hank when at last he could speak. Annette sighed contentedly and said nothing. Hank didn't ask how she felt. But from this moment, her wan and wistful demeanour vanished. She became a complete woman once more; she regained the confidence, which had prompted her many years ago to change direction away from her original inclination and into her present interest in hydroponics.

Slowly Hank realised what had happened and where he now was; he had not cared about anything for the last fifteen minutes; now he found himself stark naked in a wide passage, in a large hall flooded with light. He started fumbling for his slacks. Annette, just as naked, laughed at his obvious embarrassment, a smug satisfied look on her face. She made no effort to look away from Hank; and as the colour started to mount from his neck to the top of his head, she laughed out loud. "*Shh, Shh*, someone may hear us," cautioned an anxious Hank. Her only reply was to rise from the floor where she had been lying. She grabbed his hand and said, "Come on," and she dragged him protesting to the end of the line of shallow ponds where there was a somewhat larger one with considerably higher sides. A ladder led upwards, and she made him go before her. As she reached the top, she made a flying dive into the cool water it contained. After a brief pause, Hank followed.

Later Annette found towels on which to dry each other.

"This pool is one of our perks," she called cheerfully as she led the return for their clothes. Hank was content to follow, his eyes glued to the delightful curve of her lower back and the bobbing up and down of her Gluteus Maximus, which he had been told was the technical term used for that particular part of an anatomy. He had no use just at present for technical terms; he was spellbound by this vision that moved just in front of him.

"Everyone will be too busy learning about our future to come up here." Her assessment of the situation was quite accurate. Hank didn't realise it at the time but would come to accept, often reluctantly, that her conclusions were always perceptive and considered and what was worse after they were married, distressingly correct!

After they had dressed she continued with the tour of the Hydroponics factory farm; she started with the introduction of seedlings into the shallow end of the tanks and demonstrated how each section was gradually moved into deeper water as the plants grew larger.

"Our main task at present," she said, in a voice which had now assumed a lecture-hall precision and clarity, "is to maximise the conversion ratio. We aim to establish a system that is capable of perpetual regeneration. We will circulate the atmosphere of the entire complex through those perforated pipes that run the full length of these ponds. These plants, as long as they receive light of the correct wavelength, will absorb the C.O.2. And convert it into carbohydrates and protein, producing Oxygen as a by-product. As the plants grow they are transferred to the end of the ponds where they are automatically harvested; after a draining period they go into a unit, which separates the green leaves from the stem and root. The leaves are freeze-dried and then reformed into all the vegetables which you eat here. The stem and root are desiccated, then freeze-dried and processed into differing shapes and styles. We have a Fungi section to help with the flavouring. But when combined, this product forms the entire protein content of your diet.

"There's no wonder I've forgotten what a good steak tastes like," interrupted Hank in a grumbling tone.

"You just notice how healthy you are," retorted Annette severely. "The only inmates of our sick bay are there as a result of physical accidents, not physiological illness. We are also working towards recycling all waste products including human wastes through the same system; there will need to be a brief settling period to allow primary biological digestion to develop. We have not, as yet, ascertained the necessary area of plants required supporting each human life, but it will be straight-forward once we have a sealed environment. I've been asking Ro Stern for a date to enable us to start, but he's always evaded a direct answer. Well, I'll see what he has to say tomorrow.

Hank was utterly baffled. How could this methodical, organised, impersonal professor, speaking so confidently and business-like, be the same soft, sensual woman, who had blown all sense and care from his head less than an hour ago?

They returned to the meeting in time to hear of the proposed social arrangements, which were contemplated. When the conference had continued for six hours without pause, by general consent a proposal to continue each evening was decided upon and weary minds and bodies retired to rest.

CHAPTER FIFTEEN

"When did you get the first indication of trouble?" I asked.

"They should have checked in at 17.00 hrs," replied the transport officer, "but Dr Obas is frequently late in returning, so we didn't pay too much attention at first. Then after fifteen minutes we tried to raise him by laser-com; it has a short operational range but we expected him to be close to base and within range, but no reply. So we tried a brief call on the emergency frequency on long-range radio—still no reply. I therefore reported to Admin, at 17. 26."

An emergency call had brought Ched and me racing to the control centre to hear this report; with Pete Morgan who had joined us we anxiously discussed our options.

"We must get a search party organised straight away. We'll need a backup to follow now; where is the flight plan?"

"I've asked for it to be brought up," Pete said. "I suggest that you take Hank Hertzman with you; he's the only person on base other than Dr Obas who has regular outside travel permits. Therefore he's most likely to know where to look for them."

Dr Buzz Obas still spent much of his time indulging his passion of prospecting for a variety of minerals; this meant travelling to the Chamen Tahg foothills more than a hundred kilometres distant from Pegasus. Their transport consisted of a small four-seater anti-grav vehicle; this type of transport was used especially to provide operational experience for the designer and engineers.

I decided to lead the search with Ben Hoyt following as back up and technical adviser if required. Ched took control of the organisation base side. I hurried to my quarters for outdoor clothing knowing that it would be bitterly cold in the desert after sundown. I arrived back at the transportation departure exit at the same time as Hank who had been paged whilst he was on his way for the evening meal. Oval was on hand with an anxious expression on her face. "Ro," she said, "I've just been officially advised that our Satellite is in orbit and due to start transmitting at 21.00hrs. That's in approximately three hours from now! We had intended to carry out range and intensity testing before allowing anyone to face exposure; there is much that we are not sure of. All outside personnel have been advised to wear protective headgear at all times, but I must tell you, there has been a great deal of scepticism about the danger and we could not give a definite activation date. We've had to ask the Chinese authority to provide a launcher, then await developments; I only received positive notification at 17.30."

I was aware of Oval's concern; I knew she had suffered doubts about continuing development of the death ray. She had expressed her misgivings to me on several occasions. I had needed all my powers of persuasion to convince her to continue with the work. I reminded her that it was to ensure that the rest of the people in the base were afforded the security, which her work alone could guarantee. I was also familiar with Buzz Obas and his amused air of contempt for all authority together with his invariable laughing response and confident manner to dismiss all difficulties. I could imagine the answer to a warning of the precautionary need to wear a bulky helmet while he was digging for rock samples and I could also imagine the effect that the death of "one of our people" would have on Oval. I was very conscious of Oval's culpability neurosis occasioned by the untimely death of her husband. Beth and I had often discussed her overt symptoms of stress. Although aware of the problem, we were reluctant to intrude for fear of making matters worse and as I said, "Her work was progressing," so I accepted Beth's advice to leave well alone. However, another accident as a result of her discovery would have disastrous consequences.

As I was saying goodbye to my wife I nodded in Oval's direction; I had no need to speak; Beth would know what to do.

The anti-grav transporters were not fitted with headlights; it had never been anticipated that they would be used in the dark, so Hank and I carried powerful torches. There was no immediate need for these and we just headed due west. Hank, who had more experience of both the transporter and the terrain, was at the controls.

"If we cruise at 5 metres above the desert floor we should be well over the dunes," he said. The height of the vehicle was not affected by the rolling sand beneath us; it stayed smoothly level ignoring the occasional rocks or depressions below. It took its height as a proportion of the pull of gravity, which had its maximum effect somewhere in the earth's core.

There was little conversation between us; my stony face dissuaded conversation. I was determined to recover the exploration party and only too conscious that I had to find them first. Next to me stood the tall freckled young man with the fresh unworried appearance of a schoolboy, who drove us along with a competent and light-hearted ease. Once our eyes became accustomed to the dim starlight the undulating ground below became vaguely distinguishable. It took on a grey ghostly appearance gliding past; a silent sea of sand. There were occasional outcrops of broken rock and here where there was the slightest degree of retained moisture, clumps of thorn and cactus clawed a precarious foothold and fought to exist till the next brief rain shower. The two of us who peered ahead intently ignored the character of the desert floor on the flying platform. The helmets we wore had visors, which protected our eyes from airborne sand; the hum of the propulsion fan was almost lost in the rushing current of air as we sped toward the distant mountains. I maintained contact with base by Lasercom, which guaranteed privacy of comment until we were below line of sight. We then made occasional contact with Ben who was fifteen minutes behind us.

A little over an hour passed when Hank reduced speed to a much slower rate. The distance counter, which we had zeroed at the start of our journey, showed eighty-five km.

"We can expect higher outcrops of rock any time now," he stated confidently. I passed this information back to Ben, awaiting acknowledgement before asking, "What landmark are we looking for?"

"A longish flat top between two sharp peaks; he's been working the same area for two weeks now. I've been spot on compass bearing all the way—it should be right ahead."

Thirty minutes later I set a circular search pattern; we had seen signs of newly disturbed ground so knew we were in the vicinity of where Buzz Obas had recently been working. I glanced at my watch; there was under an hour before the death ray was due to commence operating! When Ben caught up with us I directed him to work in the opposite area to the southerly route, which we were taking. I was beginning to realise the impossible task we faced; I wondered why there was no homing signal from the emergency transmitter each craft carried. We were moving very slowly now as we cautiously approached the dimly seen rocky crags that surrounded us, and slowly rose to the top and then slowly descended the other side until we could just make out the ground below. After trying this for a while, I said to Hank, "Take her up so that we can get a wider viewpoint; we'll never get anywhere as we are doing at present." Hank backed away from the rock face and allowed our floating platform to rise higher and higher; he eventually steadied the craft at one hundred metres. Suddenly Hank shouted out!

"I can see a light! Over there." My eyes followed the outstretched arm and pointing finger, and then I too saw a faint flickering spot of brightness amid the gloom of the foothills. We immediately headed in the direction of the light with rising hopes in our hearts. Only ten minutes to go!

As we approached the faint light, we could gradually distinguish a smoky fire; it was amongst a jumble of large craggy boulders. I approved of the cautious manner in which Hank manoeuvred his craft toward the fire that even now was dying down to a few smouldering embers and had to bite my tongue to prevent crying out for more haste; but there was less than ten minutes. Now we were down below the surrounding rocks feeling our way little by little, both torches was shooting powerful beams among the harsh jagged obstacles strewn about the ground. Then I heard a faint cry and with this to guide my light I found the shiny black face of Buzz Obas.

He lay outstretched with his legs and part of his body covered with broken rock and rubble; he grinned feebly as the torchlight hit his face.

"Put her down as low as you can," I snapped. "I'll get off, then you go back up to contact Ben; tell him what the position is; you had better wait for him before you come back here." Hank gradually eased the flying platform down until he could feel it tilt as one corner came to rest against a rock, "It's the best I can manage Ro," he said.

"That will have to do then." I climbed over the edge of the platform and hurriedly lowered myself until I hung to the full extent of my arms, then let go. I had a drop of two metres onto an uneven boulder-strewn floor. My semi-bent legs absorbed my falling body weight; I staggered a couple of steps, recovered my balance, then looked up and shouted, "Okay."

I waited to see the platform begin to ascend before turning to pick my way toward Buzz who lay calmly waiting. I flashed my torch along his body until I came to the rocky covering; after a methodical look around I found a flat surface on which to rest the torch; then, by adjusting the focus so that the light spread over a wide area, I immediately set to work to strap a protective helmet onto Buzz's head I started lifting the smaller pieces of rock off the back of the fallen man. As I worked my way down the body I heard Buzz calling softly. I bent my ear close to the whispering lips. "Take it easy man; it takes very little to start them rolling again." I squeezed the brawny shoulder, "Okay, I'll be careful." I returned to a cautious removal of the football sized rocks from the body of the unmoving figure that lay still as death itself. Eventually as I cleared away the rubble and carefully placed it to one side, the cause of the injured man's inability to move was revealed;

a boulder approximately one metre in diameter lay across both his legs and feet. When I realised that I could do no more without help I returned to the big man's curly black bearded head and, lying down by his side, said, "Can you tell me what happened?" Buzz seemed to have regained some strength; his voice was clearer as he answered: "We had started for base when I caught sight of the very formation of strata that we had been searching for all week. We touched down; I told my partner to sit tight, I'd collect a quick sample to analyse tonight when we got back.

"I'd just left the platform and started walking away when the ground began to heave and shake. Then there was an almighty roar and the hillside rolled down on top of us. I turned back to the platform in time to see a boulder the size of a house land right on top of it. It seemed to stop there, jam bang on top, then there was an explosion. I imagine that was the gyro disintegrating. The rock just crumbled into a pile of rubble. I couldn't see the platform anymore; then I must have passed out. When I came round I found myself like this. I could move my head and arms and that's all. It was getting dark so I calculated that I had been out for about an hour. By the time I'd recovered my senses properly I realised that someone would come looking for us and I was trying to think of a way to attract attention. Like I said, it was getting dark and that gave me the idea; there was a thorn bush, but it was beyond my reach; after I'd finished struggling and nearly setting off another avalanche, I was frantic to get it close enough to set fire to. I had a heat gun on my belt, and then I thought of using the belt to extend my reach. The bush had been uprooted in the slide and each time I threw the belt I had visions of knocking it further down the slope; but then the buckle caught in the thorns, and I managed to drag it gradually within reach. The heat gun could easily ignite the bush but that was the only fuel I had. I thought of adding my shirt but decided to keep it on; it gets cold out here at night. So then I had an interesting calculation to work on; the bush would not burn for more than fifteen minutes, so, how long would a search party take to arrive, how long to pick up our tracks and when to light the beacon?"

"It was a close call," I admitted, "but now we're here, stop worrying." A little while later I was caught in a bright beam of light coming from the torch on board Ben's anti-grav transport. They were soon within hailing distance. "I need help to push this rock off his legs!" I yelled.

"There's no chance of landing," replied Ben.

"Okay, get as low as possible, then your partner will have to drop off."

Ben had a better idea. "We have plenty of rope, and we'll use that to climb down."

A young man soon joined me by the name of Stene; we quickly took up position at each side of Buzz's prone form and when I gave the word, heaved with all our might. The rock didn't move! Pausing only to catch our breath, we put backs to the rock, settled our feet carefully onto solid ground and again strained every muscle in a bid to move the rock from where it lay on Buzz's legs. Again, we were defeated by the inertia of the boulder. "We are not even near to moving it," I gasped. "Even with the other two, I doubt it would make much difference."

Stene made no answer; but a little later he said hesitantly, "Do you suppose we could use the anti-grav platform to take the weight?"

"How do we do that?"

"We could fashion a rope cradle around the rock, then pass a rope up to the platform to take some of the strain; then we might be able to move it over," replied Stene.

"Well, there's nothing we can use as a lever and I've nothing better to suggest, so let's give it a try." We shouted up to Ben and Hank to throw down a coil of rope and set to work. Stene knew exactly what he was doing, so I contented myself with offering a hand as required.

Buzz turned his head round to follow progress, but said nothing. Thirty minutes later the rock was surrounded with three turns of line around the circumference near to the base; then four more lines ran upwards, crossed over at the top of the rock and continued down the far side to be tied onto the circulating rope. At this stage Buzz spoke for the first time. "That rope is made of Texepropolene; if you heat it very carefully with my heat gun, it will shrink and be less likely to fall back onto my legs when you get it up a few metres. Be very careful man, or you'll turn it into treacle."

At this stage I decided to give Buzz a narcotising shot; I realised that notwithstanding no sound of complaint, Buzz's legs must be badly injured, and when the weight was removed and some sort of circulation restored to his lower limbs, there would be a merciless return of sensation.

Meanwhile maintaining control with one hand, Ben had uncoiled a further length of rope, doubled it for additional strength and passed it across the floor of his craft so that a section of line fell down each side of his platform.

Stene had climbed on top of the rock and proceeded to secure the two ends to the rope cradle.

While this was going on I took a rope hanging from

Hank's platform and arranged loops ready to attach to Buzz's big upper torso; I called up to Hank: "At the first sign of rocks sliding, take off, do you understand?"

"Yes, I can see quite well from up here."

A quick look to see that all was ready and I shouted, "It's all yours, Ben!" Ben slowly increased his lift from the almost neutral gravity, which was just sufficient to maintain his craft a few feet above the ground surface, and gradually took up the slack. At first the rope stretched and I thought that it was going to break. But then the boulder lurched to one side and a section of rope twanged across the floor of the platform as it took the full strain. The next minute the boulder was whisked off the ground following the anti-grav platform which suddenly shot up out of sight. I called to Hank: "Come in and take us up gently." The platform manoeuvred into position, then slowly ascended taking the injured body with it. Stene and I, still on the ground, eased the legs carefully from the depression, which had surrounded them for so long. "Hold it there, Hank!"

Buzz's unconscious form swung gently back and forth at the end of the line that led up to the hovering platform.

Stene and I now proceeded to place one foot each into the loops, which I had fashioned for just this purpose. With one foot each to carry our weight, we hung onto the line with one hand and used the other to steady the injured man; in this manner Hank lifted us all upwards and then carefully made his way to the nearest stretch of flat ground where he could deposit his cargo to enable us to transfer to a more comfortable position for the flight back to base.

Meanwhile Ben was having the most exciting ride of his life, as he was later to relate. He had followed the activity below, watching the ropes being lashed around the rock with a great deal of scepticism; he fully expected the ropes to pull off over the rock as he applied any sort of strain to them. He had no alternative suggestion to offer so wisely he remained silent. Now as he commenced lifting, he increased the lift very slowly waiting for the surge as the ropes slipped off. However he had failed to realise how effective the heat shrinking of the circulating cradle had been. When one of the loops of rope running down to the rock whipped across the platform deck and snatched taut in a fresh position, it caused the platform to tilt backwards; this in turn caused Ben to tighten his grip on the lift control lever; with only the briefest pause, the platform shot upwards, and the lump of rock which had so far resisted all effort to dislodge it with impunity followed with no more consequence than if it were a pebble. Fortunately a safety harness, which automatically tightened under stress, secured Ben and so he was not thrown out of the low-sided craft. The tilt of the craft and Ben's surprised unbalanced position, which he was struggling to master, made little difference to the flying platform that was now approaching 1000 metres and racing forever higher. He realised that he would soon be short of oxygen, but could not avoid speculating as to what was actually happening; if this rock, which must weigh at least a tonne, had so little effect on the lifting capacity of a thirty-centimetre gyroscope, the potential was unbelievable! Ben, who had worked on the project from the beginning, was truly astonished at what was happening and the implications, which this forced into his wondering mind. But the immediate problem was to survive; he would either freeze to death or asphyxiate if he could not regain control. The rock had thrown the craft out of balance so the overriding need was to get rid of the rock. Each vessel carried an emergency kit, which included an axe, and as his controls were of no use at present, Ben let go to concentrate on getting the axe. He chopped through the ropes; then gasped as the rope slowly parted. Instead of the rock falling away, it continued to rise with the platform!

Ben soon realised that the anti-gravity field must extend beyond the limits of the platform. Then he remembered that he was not using the propulsion fan; it had been switched off while he was hovering over the scene of the accident. Now he desperately struggled up the sloping floor of the platform to reach for and close the switch; wondering how the fan would perform in the thin air. He needed to increase the revs to maximum before he gratefully saw that he was leaving the rock behind. Then suddenly, when he estimated they were separated by a gap of ten metres, the rock fell away and vanished.

With the unbalancing effect of the rock gone, Ben quickly regained control of his craft and brought it back to earth. He found the homing signal from Hank's automatic beacon and soon joined up with the other craft from where we both made an uneventful return journey to Pegasus. This was much to the relief of several worried people who anxiously awaited our arrival.

Ched let out a quiet sigh of relief when he had completed the inventory of losses after the rescue party's return. One man missing, almost certainly dead; but until they had a body had to be referred to as missing. One anti-grav craft lost; and one man injured. From the bits of commentary passed back to base which he had heard, things might have been much worse. "I must find out who the widow is and see her to break the news before it becomes common knowledge through the grapevine," he thought. He would be glad of an excuse to get away from Patricia Obas; she had made the last two hours hell.

The fact that her husband was missing and nothing was known about why, or what was wrong, was all the fault of the head of admin. For Ched in particular and all other members within earshot, she never stopped her tirade of criticism. All the rescue party's wives were gathered around the communication desk, anxiously waiting for such news as was available.

The crucial part of the story, of finding Buzz Obas minus his partner, ensuring his protection from the death ray, recovering his trapped body from the rock slide, all had to wait until the rescuers were safely under cover; the Lasercom had only been used to announce that they were returning and occasional progress reports. We were not about to tell any searching listening station that they were out in the desert away from our protected base.

In the meantime Patricia Obas told all and sundry what a farce the whole project was; why Buzz was expected to do all the dangerous exploring, and fancy making him use a crackpot flying bedstead instead of a regular truck! She went on and on. Beth wondered how she had passed the initial entry qualifications; she vaguely remembered how she had appeared before the selection panel, as intelligent alert and extremely confident. She had been a teacher at a famous and expensive school in England, Gorton College for young Ladies. Beth smiled to herself as she tried to imagine the dismay of ex-colleagues or former students, if they could witness this harangue.

The disparagement of Ched's ability and qualifications,

the abysmal prospects for the entire project, the lack of direction in allowing her husband to work without proper protection, all poured out in a never-ending torrent of venomous abuse from the mouth of this beautiful coffee-coloured woman.

Beth thought, "How shallow is this veneer of civilisation and culture." Spilling forth now was the anguish of a tormented mind, fearful of being left alone!

Beth knew that her man was returning; she had recognised my voice before I had identified myself; at least this time I was safe. But she suffered a dread feeling of apprehension whenever I went off anywhere; she had found out that it was always Ro who led. He was always first to show what could be done. She wondered how she would react if ever she was told that Ro would not return; she didn't dwell on the thought for long—there were more immediate concerns.

That Oval was under considerable stress was amply demonstrated by her agitated striding up and down the room; she would force herself to sit down; no good, she jumped up again! Over and over she repeated to herself, "I can't take this, I can't, I won't!"

Control had received one message; a report of one man missing, presumed dead. How did he die? "If it's as a result of the particle beam, I won't live with it, I couldn't face anyone."

She had decided that she would walk out into the desert herself; without protection!

Beth made a determined effort to share these misgivings. She was well aware of the distress that Oval felt. She understood the self-doubt, the revulsion at what she had convinced herself was entirely her own responsibility.

Now Ro was standing in front of her, safe and sound, recounting our adventures, with excited interjections from a grinning Hank and a rueful Ben filling in some of the blanks. She kept a firm arm around Oval's waist, whose involuntary shivering gradually ceased as the story of the earth tremor and the rock slide was told and it became plain that the accident had occurred during daylight hours; long before the Death Ray was due to commence operating. Buzz, still unconscious, was taken to the sick bay; this had full surgical facilities and a team of surgeons glad of a problem, which appeared to offer them scope for their talents. Pat Obas had stopped raving as soon as she could see that Buzz was still breathing. Annette was there of course; she sat by his side, holding one of the large hands in both of hers as Hank made his full report. When this was concluded, they walked away arm in arm to Annette's quarters and to the general amusement of the others, (Hank's capacity for food was legendary and he had missed his dinner) were not seen again until the following day.

CHAPTER SIXTEEN

After the general meeting when the full proposals for the colonising venture were made known, when Pegasus Base became a closed and self-contained environment sealed off from the rest of Earth's inhabitants, there were many changes. The most notable was in individual personalities; all personnel had been told in general terms that the venture was specifically designed to leave Earth behind. However, when a proposal was discussed in a university library or in the course of a private dinner party or in the quiet of night in the comfort of one's own bed with a wife beside one, the sense of adventure and of being part of something entirely new and different gave a romantic and exciting air to the idea. Even in the cold light of day, when eminently sane people had seriously considered all the implications of this novel proposal and cautiously and soberly agreed to continue, there still remained a sense of unreality, despite the original detailed probing into a person's life to date, including the psychological searching through private dreams and fears. Followed by the mind draining security test before entry to Pegasus and notwithstanding the emotional preparation, which all colonists assumed that they had made and come to terms with, something had changed.

The miraculous vision of that evening was still uppermost

in the minds of many, when the astonished assembly witnessed the slow majestic ascent of the platform in the conference hall, a massive concrete structure obviously weighing many tonnes floating in thin air by some mystical means way beyond the comprehension of most of the spectators; also, the memory of the figure of Ro Stern, his arms folded across his chest, stating in that grave, harsh, voice:

"This will leave no room for debate: I am the final authority!"

This was the picture which most people present were to remember for the rest of their lives.

A statement like that was unequivocal; there was no longer the slightest doubt that an unnatural awe-inspiring event was in prospect. Emotions were galvanised into a state of agitated arousal; excitement already high became feverish: flushed bright-eyed faces looked almost unbelievingly at each other; can all this be real? When the initial exhilaration had faded and the immediate torrent of questions had been answered, the image of that floating platform and the lonely figure with the terrible voice remained forever in their minds, together with the grim statement:

"I... am the final authority."

Some simply stopped smiling; they were not unhappy or depressed, but the sheer enormity of what was proposed became believable; no one could put anything quietly out of mind, and every possibility had to be faced squarely. How could one travel for 125 years?

"I'm going to be frozen solid."

Everyone was vaguely aware that something like this was inevitable, but the magnitude of the whole concept was so far beyond belief that, like death, most put the question to one side and just refused to think about it. A twenty-tonne platform floating like a feather brought up every dark thought and demanded an answer.

For some a sense of jubilation filled them with a desire to risk life and limb. It was as if they had decided, "If I can be part of this fantastic adventure there's nothing I can't do." In an enclosed miniature world which was all they could look forward to, they could not go hang gliding, mountaineering, or sub aqua diving, the normal way of testing one's self in the outer world. But the floor levels were over ten metres between decks; so jumping off one level onto an anti-grav platform set at ever increasing depths was sufficiently foolish and dangerous to satisfy some of the younger males. For most of the community, the announcement made them into a perfect work force. Enthusiasm was without measure; everyone realised that what they were doing was a prelude to the greatest adventure of all time. They were eager to turn visions into reality. People had to be turned away from their duties and told that it was dinner time, told that a rest period was essential.

Still, the greatest solace was traditional, the traditional way of relieving excitement or stress; as ever, it was and almost certainly ever will be... Sex.

Whether it served as relief, support, or comfort.

Dr Stronberg reporting on medical matters and general health, told me, "You know that all personnel are checked for total contraception at the compulsory monthly medical; we've never known such a need for uterus flushing. I guess we've flushed away sufficient embryos to populate a dozen planets and our main prescriptive requirement is a simple salve. I tell both male and females to reduce their frequency of intercourse. But I know that they take little notice of my advice."

I didn't reply; I was thinking of my own needs, of my own requirement of Beth's body and comfort. I realised that I was only using Beth, but I was experiencing a passion that approached desperation. I wondered if I should discuss this situation with one of the shrinks. But if I did, news of this consultation was bound to leak, and what sort of effect would that have? The leader of the expedition needing psychiatric treatment! Impossible; Beth would have to serve.

Another major change was the formation of discussion groups; these were a natural development with the announcement that Project Pegasus was now fully operational. Ched Taylor had initiated proceedings by stating that once established, the new community would be subject to no existing laws.

"We must decide everything for ourselves. Now is the time to start drafting our own principles that we wish to live by. The starting point will be that everything we have when we finally land will be common property for use by the community."

Each evening a varying number of different groups gathered in the recreation hall to expound their pet theories—starting from all that was wrong with this so-called civilisation that had evolved on Earth.

As is obvious, criticism is easy, but what became ever more difficult was deciding what to replace the present system with. It is an unsubtle and simple statement to make: Thou shall not kill; Thou shall not steal…

Just assume that someone broke this simple and reasonable rule. What sanction or penalty should be imposed? Who would have authority to impose any such penalty? At this stage the laws as postulated by Plato were introduced as a possible working hypothesis, but even in those far off days communism had been regarded as impractical, and even Plato was prepared to bend his own laws of impartiality to select suitable parents for his rule by Philosophers. Socialist bureaucratic doctrines had failed a century ago and everyone could witness the unbridled capitalism of today. Minimum government is a fine principle, but who would construct the pipeline to take water to the new settlement or build the power plant, or the new dwellings required for the progeny that will surely gush from long barren wombs once control of reproduction was lifted?

The need for values is inbred. Their content is not. That need is driven by an innate moral sense in most people. Part of the innate moral code is a sense of what is just and proper. This built-in necessity is the basis of laws that govern all societies. The planned expedition could at least start their adventure from a base free from the colour and cultural bias, which has been such a tragic feature of Earth's history. The outstanding attribute of this multiracial group was intelligence. An intelligent individual holds neither nationalistic nor racial prejudice; one looks for and admires similar abilities in others. But what is goodness? Good qualities are those that draw us to others and which we wish to be credited with ourselves. But goodness implies hard work and sacrifice. Who would we entrust with making a decision for the help required by the deserving? Or ourselves when we needed help.

Slowly and painfully a few basic principles emerged and were accepted, with all personnel providing an individual signature.

This was the first law to become law; any rule must be

unanimously accepted. Rule two was that all property over and above strictly personal domestic possessions would revert to the community at death. It was thought that this would contain natural capitalist inclinations and eliminate the need for general taxation. Rule three: no weapons of any kind would be allowed. Rule four: there was to be no restrictions other than self-imposed on stimulants or drugs in any form. It was foreseen that medicinal drugs would need to be developed; but to keep them purely for medicinal purposes would require additional rules and enforcement. This then would be an encroachment on individual liberties, therefore was not acceptable. A fascinating develop-ment from this discussion led to the question of censorship. If speech and dress and literature are to be uncensored, so must pornography, acting, or prostitution.

The second evening of this discussion had attracted a large vociferous gathering. Among the crowd was Curt Jurgens, the spokesman for the Swiss robotic-specialist engineers recruited from help unlimited. After a while Curt stood up to ask for a hearing; he was tall and slim, he wore no artificial hair, his scholarly pate shone in the overhead lighting. Very few people had had an opportunity to speak with Curt and his friends, so all were curious to hear what he had to say.

"I wish to draw your attention to an aspect of our work of which you may not be aware; I'm sure I can show you something of interest which will contribute to our discussion." He continued his remarks with a smirk on his lips. "If you will just bear with me for a moment..." He brought out a small music box which he placed it on the floor and set it playing.

A beautiful soulful melody filled the air; it was music with a difference. In a quiet peaceful way it demanded attention; there was a haunting air with an insistent drumming vaguely in the background; its challenging cadenzas held all who heard it spellbound. Eva leaned towards Ched and whispered, "That's the best synthesised music I've ever heard; I'll bet it was composed by computer—just listen to the progression of the minor key!"

Uncharacteristically Curt's companion that evening was an attractive dark haired girl who appeared to be in her early twenties. Unusual, because the three Swiss normally kept very much to themselves and never associated with females.

Noted by the few trained musicians in the audience, after two minutes there was a change of rhythm; whereupon, the dark girl gracefully rose to her feet and started to dance to the music.

It was a totally different dance form to any which had been witnessed by those present. Her legs glided and slid across the floor and before anyone realised how, she had turned and was slipping back in another direction; her slim body swayed from side to side forming elegant arcs with her legs; her arms undulating like the branches of a willow tree in a gentle breeze. Her dress was a lemon coloured mass of chiffon; as she turned   the dress floated out in an elegant circle; then she would effortlessly leap into the air to land on the toes of one foot; the briefest pause rock steady, then she would sweep around the floor again. Another increasingly more noticeable change in tempo: the drumming became more insistent, the dancer reached to the collar of her dress and continued with her dance, but now as she moved around the floor her dress began to slide slowly down from its original position. Eva once more murmured to Ched, and Ched didn't answer; his attention was fully occupied with the entertainment being provided. Right now he was fascinated by the manner in which the dress slid tantalising from her shoulders as though it was on invisible strings. Each time she twisted the dress slipped a little lower, but did not collapse altogether. The music became louder, faster, the drumming more insistent; the dancer increased her pace to match. The upper torso of the dancer was now completely naked. Then, with a last tremendous leap high into the air, the dancer must have been nearly a metre above the floor, and the dress was left behind like a huge flower on the floor. The Venus-like figure of the dancer landed, again on her toes. She stood perfectly still like a statue of mellow marble. Her figure was as perfect as any artist could dream of. It was the figure of a nymph, with the bloom and fullness of breast and buttocks that normally occurs in a newly pregnant female. The music faded into a calm stillness.

The audience was stunned into perfect silence; and then after a moment, spontaneous applause broke out. The dancer slowly moved towards her dress, stepped into the centre and with a smooth and nonchalant motion lifted the dress into its normal position. Then, without a word, she resumed her seat by Curt's side.

As the applause died away Curt stood up and, with a smile on his lips, said, "I expect you realise 'Anthea' here is an android. It occurred to us that as we have been discussing the sort of entertainment we must consider when we are away from earth, because our numbers are to be limited to approximately four hundred, we will very possibly be short of entertainment, especially when you think of the range we are accustomed to at present. Even if as Eva wishes, we become reasonably proficient with musical instruments, when we have seen and heard the entire stock of tapes that we will be able to carry with us, there is going to be a shortage of artistic and harmonious tradition to support us. If we are to reject so much of earth's culture, we will need to develop our own. I suggest that the demonstration, which we have just witnessed, could contribute to our future entertainment requirements. There could be many extensions to this basic idea. I see no reason why we should not operate a house or several houses or possibly theatres of pleasure; staffed and operated entirely by androids. Of course, you will have noted that Anthea's genitalia are not complete; it was considered inappropriate at the present time. However, that can easily be changed when and if required, and as we are to establish an egalitarian society, cosmetic male organs are just as simple to provide."

Ben Hoyt who was seated with his friend Si Lucas, let out a low whistle. "Those birds don't say much but when they do, can they sing! I wonder what my wife will have to say about his last remarks."

There was a general, somewhat uneasy pause in the proceedings; even today people felt a little embarrassed by the clinical manner in which Curt had spoken about Anthea's body. Looking at the dark haired beauty by Curt's side, it was difficult to think of her as a machine. Anthea sat quite still, legs crossed and hands clasped in her lap, a gentle smile on her lips, her eyelids occasionally blinking with her eyes demurely lowered.

I was wondering what other kind of androids these three peculiar men had contemplated!

CHAPTER SEVENTEEN

As Pegasus was completely sealed from the outside world, a routine slowly developed which helped the prospective voyagers come to terms with their expected future. It was quite obvious that no one had the slightest doubt of achieving the target that was proposed. However, this left the people who were always referred to as support personnel increasingly restive; their future was to be on this world and they wished to return to it as soon as possible. But some were infected with the air of excitement that was prevalent everywhere in all discussions and all activities. They became another problem to arrive on my desk; some of them were asking to be allowed to join the expedition. By the time the new volunteers had been screened through the Personal Minimum Necessary Requirement programme, they were reduced to no more than thirty-three. The first complication was that there were only nine females among them, and that left me with a dilemma, for I was bound by the original constitution. This called for a company of equal numbers of male and female members. Oval however had always upset that balance from day one. Then, as events proved, people have a habit of dying unexpectedly and as it was more often males who died first and earlier in life, a slight surplus of male personnel to compensate for the mortality rate was deemed a prudent change of formula.

Two of the applicants were easily accepted. Hank was one; he also asked if I would perform a joining ceremony between Annette and himself.

But a big surprise for me and for others was the second application.

It was from Mac, the man who because of his grizzled greys hair and obvious mature years stood out from the youthful majority who surrounded him in Pegasus and made him the butt of much good humoured chaffing. He also made a request for a joining ceremony, to Oval Himnal!

This proposed union attracted widespread interest; both parties were well known throughout the base and although they were frequently seen together the prospect of them marrying caused quite a stir. Mac had always intended to marry, but he never stayed in one place for very long; then another offer of interesting work always proved more seductive than the particular female he had become attracted to. He was greatly flattered when he realised that Oval was quite serious about wishing to live with him. How could he not be? He was forty-three years old and nothing to look at, as he was the first to admit. Oval was tall and athletic, a blonde-haired Germanic beauty not yet thirty; but she knew what she wanted. She wanted Mac and she knew how to get him. Beth and Eva were discussing the situation and decided that Oval was looking for a father figure, someone to lean on. They burst out giggling at the image conjured up of the big blonde leaning too heavily on the slight Scot. I confided to Ched, "Well, at least we should be able to construct our quarters on the new world if Hank and Mac are to go with us." So some of the in-house romance had a happy ending with this demonstration of how normal social life was developing in the new organisation.

The evening discussions continued and it soon became apparent that to formulate a society without restrictions or formal government was no easy matter; for instance, how should control of exuberant young people be exercised? A strongly favoured suggestion was that at eighteen years of age all adolescents should serve for two years in a pioneer force. It was assumed that there would always be suitable projects to absorb the excess of young vigour that would forever demand an outlet at this age. Then two years apart from one's family would prove to be sound disciplinary training, a beneficial break before continuing with strenuous advanced, technical educational instruction. The whole social structure would be family based; parents would be responsible for their own offspring's education until the age of eighteen. A universal curriculum was to be formulated and an annual examination would ensure that a minimum standard was achieved. Each family would be responsible for maintaining their older relatives who could no longer do this for themselves. The overriding principles were to be self-reliance, with tolerance for the less able; independence from bureaucratic interference, the right to live as one wished and to die when one chose. The last item was to accommodate the frequently expressed demand for "The right to die." Hank was bewildered after the first general meeting when he had been so gloriously seduced by his new wife; he had become a regular at the evening deliberations. He attached the utmost importance to increasing his understanding of the ideas, which this peculiar organisation was hammering out. He was especially concerned by his lack of formal qualifications; here he was, married to a professor who was entitled to add any number of letters after her name and he could not even put engineer to his signature.

For the second time in his young life Hank suffered from fits of depression. When his Mother had died, he found solace in hard physical activity; now instinctively he grasped for relief by total immersion in a previously uncared for occupation. He became a regular in the base library; he wanted to know what meritocracy meant. He wanted to read about the theories of Marx, Engels, Smith and Mann.

He had lived in a mildly Christian household throughout his early years, but now he heard phrases like, "Priests were the first deluder's of mankind." He wondered why so many of his new companions were contemptuous of religion. Although he read for hours and slowly acquired a vast background of historical facts and in his day-to-day duties he enquired why and how, his mind could not understand most of the technical explanations that were freely offered. It was to be twenty years later when he was elected to be the first FIRST PERSON of the community of VIRGENA that he ceased to worry over his shortage of qualifications.

In the meantime he listened to, but made no contribution to debates on the minimum level of education necessary before a couple would be allowed to bear children. Would the venturers be expected to make a contribution to the new society, or could they lead their own independent lives without concern for anyone else? The more Hank heard, the more bewildered he became; he had not thought that life could be so complex. He heard opinions about life on Earth that he had never considered; for example, how the immense and increasing population was polluting and poisoning their existing environment by their very numbers.

Again, how over the previous century international business had blossomed and matured so fruitfully that it dominated all aspects of life on Earth. Nowhere was this more apparent than in the entertainment industry, which now was the strongest rival to replace religion for the dubious honour of becoming the opium of the masses. Since the advent of cheap power, relatively few people bothered to increase their knowledge. If work was no longer necessary, why trouble with education? It was much more fun to surf and chase girls. Many girls held similar views; a few hours helping in the local hotels or shops would buy food and clothes, which were both cheap and plentiful.

Listening to these discussions depressed Hank; he had been happy with his life and after the initial passion and excitement of holding Annette's slim form in his arms each night had moderated, he considered himself the most fortunate man on earth. Now the realisation of how hollow life was becoming on this world and having doubts about his ability to achieve the minimum level of education which was being vigorously proposed as a requirement on the new world, threw him into black moods of despair. Annette to whom he admitted his fears assured him he was being silly; she said, "I would never have married a dumpling."

Hank wasn't so sure; the next minute Annette threw her arms around his neck, kissed him hard, then just as he felt his blood start to tingle and desire begin to stir, she slipped away from him. "I'll race you to the pool!" she yelled, then scooted into an elevator slamming the door before he could follow.

It was later when, blissfully content, they were returning arm in arm to their room, that they heard the explosion!

"What on earth was that?"

Hank was first to act. "Come on, whatever it was we've got to get down fast." They were on the top level among the hydroponic ponds; that meant six sections of escape chutes to negotiate to get out.

Annette was soon off the mark, racing for the chute; a cardinal rule was never to use the elevators in any emergency. Hank barely managed to grab her before she flung herself onto a chute mat. "Have you forgotten?" he shouted at her frantically. "A helmet! A helmet!"

Annette was amazed at this display. He had grabbed at her tunic including some of the flesh beneath, but the pain she felt was quickly ignored as she saw the dismay on Hank's face. He snatched up one of the helmets from the rack at the head of the chute and virtually rammed it onto her head, and then fastening the chinstrap he allowed her to jump onto the mat and away.

He had to pause; his chest was heaving, and he took massive breaths to try to relieve the terror that overcame him! Then fastening a helmet securely onto his own head, he followed down the chute. At each floor it became necessary to halt, pick up the mat and take a few steps to the next chute. It was floor three before Hank could think clearly again. He had once witnessed the discovery of a would-be intruder to the complex and would never forget the grisly look of agony on the face. For the past thirty seconds he had imagined Annette's face with that look on it; this thought which refused to disappear, caused such dread as to leave him numb in mind and body.

Everyone started to gather on the admin level; the general alert had not sounded, nor had the evacuation siren.

I stood with Ched and Pete by the duty communication officer waiting for information. While we waited with mounting anxiety, I asked Pete, "Any progress with the unauthorised entry report Pete?"

"There are ten people actually authorised and certified competent to sustain the generator complex," replied Pete Morgan. "I use the term *sustain* deliberately. It's not a machine in the true sense of the word; it seems that it works without anyone really understanding how! Excepting Kratsky, of course. It starts with a bottle of Hydrogen at one end and converts this into just as much electricity as is demanded at the other, apparently without limit. There are no wheels, no furnace, no pipes, just lots and lots of wires, and a damned big heavy box in the middle."

"I read a paper once on the principles involved," I stated. "It's called electro-magnetic plasma stripping, but that's as much as I know. How are you doing in finding a potential saboteur?"

"Well, I've eliminated you and Ched.

"It seems that Ched, received a video call from his old university in California, offering some information he'd asked for. They wanted to negotiate a swap, so Ched needed to get your approval at 0300hrs; you were both under direct observation by the communication officer until 0400. I'm still awaiting replies to my enquiries on most of the others, but these things take time." With that reply, I had to contain my anxieties as best I could.

The lighting suddenly increased in brightness and then went out, plunging everywhere into inky darkness. The emergency lighting took over immediately, followed by a harsh voice on the intercom.

"Matt Gronberg calling from the generator house, can you hear me?"

The duty officer quickly reassured him; then Matt continued, "I was opening the door to the power house when

Devlin Bhutto rushed through nearly knocking me over; he ran towards the transportation park. I started to follow when the explosion occurred. I turned to look. After a few seconds I could see that the lights were still on so I went back to see what had happened!"

Pete was among the waiting group. He struck his palm with his fist as he heard the name of Devlin Bhutto. He was still considering what to do about the information he had received; in this place he had no guards to call on; security here consisted of himself, a deputy and one clerk. Should he have anticipated Bhutto's action? How could he? There was nothing definite to go on, just an uneasy feeling, a hunch.

"Well, what's the damage?" snapped Ched.

There was a distinct pause.

"Are you still there?"

"Yes, I'm still here but I'm not staying! The gas governor is kaput! I don't know how it's happened but the magnetic valve that controls the fuel supply seems to have disintegrated and there's no limit to the hydrogen feed!"

"What does that mean?" I asked quickly.

"It means that the entire converter will get hotter and hotter until it melts! Unless the hydrogen container explodes first!"

"Stay here Ched; I'll go and look. See if you can get chief Kratsky to join me down there..."

The heat coming from the doorway of the generation hall could be felt as soon as I entered the corridor. The inside of the power-house was as hot as an oven; it was flooded with nitrogen gas that was supposed to smother any normal fire, but it had no effect on what was happening here; it takes more than nitrogen to kill a hydrogen reaction. So much for safety planning, I thought.

After a few words with the highly-strung disbelieving chief engineer, I called Ched.

"Full emergency evacuation, Ched!" I cried, "And don't hang about outside. You'll need to be at least five kilometres away if this thing goes up!"

Before I had finished speaking I could hear the wail of the siren.

"So we have a runaway reactor," I said, "surely there must be a way to switch it off?"

The chief engineer snarled his reply, "All output is related to the quantity of Hydrogen fed to the reactor. The only hope is to cut off the fuel supply. You can see the main outlet valve from the pressure vessel is already hot, there is smoke coming from the gland; it will be so hot that I'm not sure we could move it even if we could reach it."

"What about the fire suits?"

"When I open the door have a look for yourself!" The chief pulled open the heavy metal door that opened into the power house; a blast of skin blistering heat caused everybody to stagger backward. I lay on the floor with one hand just above my eyes, to look inside the inferno towards the massive generator; I had to hold my breath against the flood of Nitrogen that gushed out. What I could distinguish was the central block which was glowing a dull angry red; then nearer to the door I saw what I was looking for—the squat round shape of the liquid hydrogen container. A menacing stillness belied its terrible potential for destruction. A coiled tube emerged from the top to snake its way to the centre of the generator. I quickly withdrew; the chief slammed the iron door shut to restrain the overpowering flood of heat.

The chief was yelling: "There's a simple open and shut

cock at the neck of the bottle, but I can't see anyone; even with a fire suit on to reach it, even then it's probably so hot that it will be stuck in its open position. All we can do is run for it!" I was calculating the limited options open when Curt interrupted my train of thought.

"What on earth are you doing here?" was my first response.

"I think that we can help," replied Curt. "D.O.X.5. here could turn that cock off."

The chief engineer, Matt Gronberg and I, all stared at Curt.

He merely repeated, "I heard what you were saying and I'm telling you that this Android can easily perform the task you described."

All present turned to stare at Paul, who was just behind Curt's figure. He alone showed no distress in the enervating heat that filled the corridor.

I quickly decided, "If you think it's possible, go ahead."

The chief engineer who had retreated further down the passage in an attempt to avoid the heat advancing through the door shouted, "The lever stands at twelve-o-clock, it needs a 90 degree turn to three-o-clock, to shut off the gas."

Curt turned to face Paul, spoke a few words which I could not hear, then opening the door, pointed inside the inferno and stood to one side.

Paul strode into the furnace that the powerhouse had now become. It was twenty metres to the steps that led up to a gantry, which ran the circumference of the Hydrogen sphere. Ten metres inside, Paul's tunic was smouldering; as he reached the foot of the steps his clothes burst into flames. So much I could see before being forced to turn my head away from the impossible fury. My next view of events was of Paul with both arms raised to apply maximum effort to turn the lever at the neck of the Hydrogen container. I saw the arms come down to stop the lever at right angles. I wished that my view had stopped there, but it did not. The hands on the lever were already black and shapeless; fortunately I couldn't see Paul's face for the next minute; the entire figure collapsed into a heap of smoking cinders. Curt, without comment or show of emotion, slammed the door shut.

CHAPTER EIGHTEEN

The evacuation siren started its hateful bawl. All personnel who had been issued with a security pass automatically registered on the display in a green L.E.D. which was above the only exit. As each person left Pegasus, their display changed to red. Pete glanced up and he noted two numbers were already at red. "The Bhuttos," he snarled, "I'll bet my life on it." But now his job was to see that everyone left the building quickly. The communication officer was on the public address system, broadcasting throughout the whole complex,

"Leave the building as quickly as possible; do not forget your helmets, do not assemble outside, you must move well away from this building." Pete watched the display; whole blocks were switching to red. Soon there were less than twenty numbers left, but his eyes were riveted to one that was rapidly alternating between green and red; suddenly alone on the screen, this number became a blank, black, void.

Then over the intercom Ro's voice: "Okay Ched, we've done all we can down here, see you outside."

Ched sent the communication officer out and waited to see his number change to red; there were only two green lights left. "That must be you and me Pete, let's get out." They ran across to the chute, strapped on helmets and banged down onto mats. They were soon outside, then ran across to join the rest of the party with me. Here, the chief engineer in a cracked excited voice was shouting, "We must run! If that bottle blows up there will be debris dropping for many kilometres. I tell you we must get right away." We collected a few stragglers on the way who had slowed until they saw the chief running. Eventually we arrived at a deeper depression in the dunes and here we stopped exhausted, and waited!

It was only then that we started to collate the sequence of events which had caused us to leave our comfortable living quarters and to flee to this desolate spot, to huddle together in the bitterly cold desert.

Pete started by saying, "I've been getting back replies to my enquiries on all powerhouse pass-key holders. I asked for full details, about where they had gone, what was known about their families, what had happened to their possessions, in short any information that was available."

"Do you mean that you have been poking about in my affairs?" asked the chief in an angry voice...

I quickly interrupted to say, "I told Pete to check out thoroughly all personnel with access to the power house. We had to try to find out who made an unauthorised entry during the night."

"It would appear to have been the Bhuttos," groaned Pete in a bitter tone. "I didn't take sufficient care. I received a puzzling reply regarding some property in Capri. It was registered to Devlin Bhutto and local taxes were still being met. I couldn't locate him when I called, so I left a message on his phone asking him to call me. That was a mistake. I didn't really suspect anything, and I was expecting a simple explanation. Anyway, he must have been ready to strike—it didn't take him long to make his escape plans. Just before I heard the explosion there was a report from transport to say that a man down there was unconscious and a Jeep was missing. I suppose that his wife went there; few people would suspect harm from a woman—she could get quite close to the man and then give him a shot from a gas gun. But they must have interfered with the warning system because no indication that a door was being opened came through to the control desk."

"Remember they were both electricians."

"Aye, and a clever one, I'll give him that—he had talent," the chief admitted. "Undoubtedly, they will be well away by now."

The next hour was spent huddled tightly together, trying to contain what little heat we could. When the expected explosion failed to occur, we fell to discussing our next move. A little later the two engineers, with Hank and I, made a reluctant start back towards the huge semi-spherical building that dominated the bleak landscape.

We entered by the only portal at first floor level.

Inside, the dim emergency lighting cast an eerie green glow that did nothing to lessen the apprehension that filled each man's thoughts.

The chief made no bones about what could happen if ten tonnes of liquid hydrogen escaped the confines of its pressurised container. Descending by the stairs that lay alongside the elevator shafts, we opened the door at the foot; heat met us like an opening furnace door.

"If we open the door to the generator house it will only make matters worse," I said, "so we'll make a start without looking inside."

I led them to the workshop area. While Hank and Matt

laboriously opened the door to the transport garage by hand, I, together with the chief, went searching for the tools that we had decided on. We took two anti-grav cars, then slowly made our way to the top of the powerhouse roof. Here, twenty metres apart, each team started to drill. The chief said, "The roof thickness is .5 metre; don't drill too far in, just over halfway should be okay." I took one drill and Hank the other. Ten minutes later we inserted expanding eye bolts into the holes and tightened them up. "We'll have two in each section," said the chief. Next a cable was passed over the floor of each car and secured to the eyebolts.

"Now for the easy part," laughed Hank; no one joined in with his laugh. I took one of the sonic disintegrators and Hank the other. I was thinking that Hank hadn't a care in the world, whereas I had to contend with deep seated worries about the international forces being directed against China; I realised that the loss of the power plant must delay the construction of the ship by many months. For how long would Ho Chek be prepared to continue his support? This gloomy speculation dominated my thoughts as I struggled to master the settings of the disintegrator.

"If you keep at least a metre away from the hooks," said the chief, "and keep the field control on minimum, it should be safe." Kratsky was thinking, "That young flea brain hasn't the faintest idea of the forces bottled up underneath us!" Kratsky was only too well aware of the potential destructive energy which the building contained. He could not but worry at his thoughts regarding the conditions, which must apply within this gigantic bell jar below. He wondered how he had been foolish enough to be in his present predicament; but it had been his idea to release the overpowering heat which had built up within the power-house by opening relief ports at the top of the structure; so here he was, stuck in a flimsy contraption secured by a wire cable to a potential bomb. Sweat ran from his sloping forehead down his long nose to drip from the end. He brushed at it angrily with the back of his hand.

The disintegrators were normally used for breaking rock at the cement works. They were being used now to avoid the risk of sparks which would be caused by a disc saw or a laser which would have been the normal choice of tool to cut a hole in the thick concrete roof. It took a little while to find the correct width and angle of attack, but soon we got the hang of it. The concrete started to crumble into a broken crude looking strip at our feet as we worked backwards. I was thinking, I hope Hank has enough sense to leave some support! We were literally cutting the floor from beneath our feet; I left a short section unbroken at the end of every metre I travelled. My back ached and my arms were numb from the vibration, but at least I had no time to worry about what might happen if an explosion occurred right now. Chief Krastsky, controlling the platform directly above me, was a nervous wreck; not only could he imagine an explosion occurring any minute, but he also worried about the consequences of pulling a plug out of the roof of a building filled with nitrogen and hydrogen gas heated to unknown temperatures. Then hardly daring to think, what would be the result when fresh air and oxygen entered? He didn't need to be a chemist to know that Nitrogen and Hydrogen were intrinsic components of T.N.T.!

I rested my disintegrator to move across to see how Hank was progressing. I was a little embarrassed to find Hank ready for the final cutting of the supporting sections.

"There's no suggestion of the centre giving way," Hank stated, "I think it's safe to cut the last sections but then if it still remains stuck, how much lift can we exert from the platforms?"

We continued to crumble the last sections until the full circle was completed. "The problem is that there's no lateral free space for the broken concrete to move into and once it's cracked right through the sonic energy just dissipates into the void below," I said. "I can only suggest that we extend the broken area at one end of the plug; sooner or later the broken pieces must fall." This suggestion meant another hour of labour; then the anti-grav platforms took a turn; a straight pull upwards did nothing except threaten to bend the floor of the platforms. I noticed a slight movement of the plugs however, so I called to the chief, "Try vibrating it loose with small surges, being careful, remembering Ben Hoyt's experience of lifting heavy rocks!" Hank and I quickly abseiled down the side of the building; we had been conscious of weight-loss as we came within the magnetic field range of the anti-grav platforms. If they were to try shaking the plugs loose with variations of power levels, Hank and I had no intention of being anywhere near to run the risk of being sucked up when the plugs came out. We hurried away from the foot of the Powerhouse to a position that enabled us to see the effect of the anti-grav cars' endeavours.

Chief engineer Kratsky was not a happy man; he had been pleased when Ro and Hank volunteered for the concrete breaking operation; but now it was his turn. His problem was a highly active imagination; he had imagined the roof collapsing under the pounding of the disintegrators; this hadn't happened but now he was expecting to be blown to kingdom come. He thought, "When I feel it move I'll pull to one side. I'll not be on top of it." His craft needed a great deal of momentum to have any discernable effect on the giant plug of concrete he was trying to dislodge. However, his previous tugging had finally shaken loose the broken and crumbled concrete, which had been holding everything tight, and he remained unaware of this. He shouted into the intercom to the second car, "The next pull we'll make the last—make it a good one!" He adjusted his lift control to force eight on the ten point scale. The chief was scared and angry; he was angry because of his fear; he now threw the lever over savagely. His platform, now that the plug was free, went zooming skywards; the concrete plug floated out like a feather and accompanied the platform; by fortunate coincidence or not, the second platform followed... Hank and I then had a ringside seat to the most amazing spectacle.

As the two apertures suddenly appeared in the roof of the powerhouse, the superheated gases it contained erupted into the night sky. Propelled by terrific internal pressure, the twin columns of hot gases quickly caught up to the magnetic field generated by the fleeing platforms. This immediately transmuted the gas into two shafts of green writhing luminescent energy providing an astonishing pyrogenic display.

"That will be visible for a hundred kilometres," I gasped.

"I'll bet the Bhuttos think they've succeeded in blowing us all to hell!"

CHAPTER NINETEEN

Many more eyes than the Bhutto's saw the brilliant towering columns of green gas.

The spectacle lasted for less than a minute, but this was sufficient time to arouse the curiosity of three aircraft crews who were within a hundred Kilometres radius of Pegasus and many citizens of Suchou, the nearest sizeable settlement. One of the aircraft made a violent change of direction, as the drowsy pilot imagined the green pencil of light to be aimed directly at his plane. The consequential disturbance to his passengers ensured hundreds more pairs of eyes became observers; the airwaves crackled with angry radio requests for explanation and reassurance.

The Chinese military naturally denied everything, but world press was quick to ask embarrassing questions. They were awaiting the arrival of the aircraft on landing to make attractive offers for stories and the few video pictures secured by two fast-acting cameramen on board.

All this led to unwelcome attention for everyone connected with the venture. During the course of denials, one nervous official spokesman let slip the name "Pegasus".

The press were buzzing like wasps round a honeypot, but the Chinese military were both efficient and noted for harsh treatment for trespasses on military property, inevitably classing all reporters as spies.

Although Pegasus was crippled by the destruction of their power plant, its defences were not impaired. This was to be twice demonstrated before the danger of flying too low and close to the complex was finally accepted. Two small, low flying picture-seeking planes crashed sickeningly into the bleak desert as they flew within range of the defence system which multiplied the normal gravitational attraction of earth by an innumerable factor.

Secrecy however was finished; the world now knew that something of an extraordinary nature was being attempted in the heart of the Sin Kiang desert—known to some at least as PEGASUS!

The worldwide excitement had no effect on the adventurers who were the subjects of it all. It was daylight before all returned to Pegasus. Here they found a hive of activity; search-parties were organised to pick up stragglers, and teams were being formed to bring back into service the discarded portable generators which had been put to one side once the unlimited resources of the Hydro-Magnetic plant was available. But the prime endeavour was to discover how much damage had been caused in the powerhouse. Chief Engineer Kratsky was making a report on this to me two days later.

"The first observation I must make is that we are unable to resolve the sequence of events in any manner which will lead to a satisfactory explanation of the situation that we have found."

I prepared myself to listen to the long-winded exposition that all experts appeared unable to avoid when asked for an opinion. So I waited.

Kratsky, all the tension and fear he'd displayed on the roof of the powerhouse forgotten, soon found his natural pompous braying tone. "We have agreed that the fuel governor was deliberately destroyed by some sort of short-circuiting arrangement."

Again, I waited without comment,

Kratsky continued: "This allowed an excess of raw material to the reactor tunnel. What happened next is open to debate, but I am certain that the magnetic field maintained functional integrity. The weakness was in the collecting grid and sub-sequent conductors; these components were inadequate to accommodate the inevitable increased voltage developed in the vortex. If you remember, this was demonstrated by the increased brightness of the lighting before it overloaded."

"Yes, I remember."

"We have no way of measuring the quantity of hydrogen which would have been converted into plasma," Kratsky continued, "but heat was produced once the conductors failed to remove the current generated; this had to go somewhere, so every piece of metal in the immediate vicinity became a capacitor and when overloaded started to radiate. However, the most remarkable circumstance is the condition of the insulation!"

"What is so special about that?" I enquired.

"Well, all modern insulating materials are a compound of Guar, which has a molecular number of...."

"Spare me the details," I interrupted, "just tell me the outcome."

"Well, somewhere along the line the Guar has meta-morphosed into a Silicate form; this of course has enhanced incandescence stability and..."

"So what does that mean?" I was trying hard not to shout.

There was a line of people waiting to see me on various aspects of the complex that would require decisions and reassurances and I was anxious to make a tour of the entire building to get the feel of how the community were reacting to the recent emergency. However, the next words were reward for my forbearance.

"It means that instead of having to replace the entire power generating unit as I had anticipated, if we renew the collectors and main conductors, which we can construct within our own facilities to a greater capacity, of course, I expect to be able to restart the generator and operate it at a much improved level of efficiency!"

I little realised that this reassuring information was as much part of Kratsky's vivid imagination as his earlier fears when employed as part of the relief operation on the powerhouse roof—imagination, which enabled a high intelligence to visualise the possibilities of radically changed circumstances. It was this combination of acute observation allied to comprehension that made Kratsky undisputed leader of his field. My main conclusion was, "What a pity he is not as concise as he is competent."

Much later that day I made time to visit the workshop to find out what effect the evacuation had had on progress to the prototype spaceship programme.

Ben soon reassured me. "We have our own power supply, which only delayed us by the one day required to decommission a spare genny. Of course the casting bay is at a standstill."

I passed on the good news that Kratsky expected to replace the main supply in a matter of days rather than the months, which everyone had been resigned too.

Ben said, "I can't stand his company socially, but there's no doubting his abilities. We can continue our immediate work with the power supply, which is available here. We are preparing the interior surface of the sections that make the shell of the craft to receive the Lithium coating. We've decided to deposit it by electrolytic diffusion. The finer the degree of attenuation we can achieve, the faster retrieval we realise. We propose testing the capacitance of three separated layers."

Ben was referring to the emergency power supply for the Spaceship; the theory was to convert the whole of the remote internal surface area into a giant electrical accumulator. Nothing had been found to better Lithium for this purpose. "We'll use Guar to insulate the layers of course and when you think that there will be over a thousand sections to form the upper shell and an equal number for the lower one, you will appreciate the area we have available is colossal. It will set a record for being the largest battery in the world until we leave anyway. Assuming we can continue without further interruptions, the next major operation will be the outer shield. I'm anticipating difficulties there."

The difficulties arose from the catalysing action of light!

"The tests which we have run on the stuff show that even low light levels initiate the reaction. We must devise a method of spraying the entire surface in one operation in complete darkness."

Ben was reflecting on another product, which had been discovered and developed on site by a co-operative effort of Teng Ho and Bus Obas. Their combined talents were mainly responsible for a surface coating, which had the property of becoming harder than diamond! It was proposed to cover the entire outer surface with this material if a suitable method of application could be devised; then the action of ultraviolet light would change the molecular structure to form an entirely novel material. It was said to be harder than diamond because diamond would not scratch it and no other test had yet been devised. If successful, this product should prove invaluable in protecting the ship from the thousands of miniature meteorites we would inevitably encounter on our journey through space! The ablation of the surface of the spaceship was one of the many hazards that the designers had foreseen; without the benefit of this novel technique, a substantial additional thickness of material would be needed to compensate for the loss.

"When we have the surface protection problem resolved, we will be ready for the Particle drive unit, but that's in the hands of the drive physicists. I can't speak with any authority on that, it's way out of my competence. I can understand the principles, but not the actual mechanics. Oval was trying to illustrate the significant aspects of the theory to me last week; I hadn't realised that she was a student with Professor Sansung in Tokyo working on her postgraduate studies. She has renewed their connection now. That's where she met her first husband and it was an oddity in their calculations that they were trying to eliminate, which gave them the clue to the brain-destroying properties of anti-photons. She's a different person and much happier now that she's working on a constructive project. To explain as simply as I can, the Sansung drive gathers available hydrogen atoms in so-called empty space; I suppose you will remember that there is approximately one hydrogen atom in every cubic centimetre, along with other bits and pieces left over from the Big Bang; this will be more than enough for our needs. The drive gathers hydrogen and by fusion, converts it into mass and anti-matter. The mass is ejected at one end of the drive and the anti-matter is induced to the leading edge of the craft, in this manner producing a sort of suction effect. We have to carry a supply of hydrogen to start the system up and to overcome inertia once we are out of the effective range of Earth's gravitational field. That's a figure of speech, of course; we will always be subject to gravity from one source or another, but as the attraction of gravity is inversely proportional to distance, the effect in our particular case will be negligible. Then there is the bonus that low gravitation enhances the efficiency of the magnetic field strength required for the fusion process."

This talk was becoming too technical for me, so with a few words of support I left.

My next call was to the hospital to see Buzz Obas.

Buzz had arrived in hospital with both his lower legs cruelly crushed and mangled; this was a result of not running fast enough when an earth tremor disturbed the rocks on a mountain side. His running too slowly was his personal version of events and like much of Buzz's commentary, not to be taken too seriously.

It was just four weeks since Buzz had had his difference of opinion with a boulder; the main trouble he had suffered was comminuted fracture injuries to the Tibia of both legs, together with similar injuries to Metatarsal and associated bones in his feet! In earlier times a monotonous four to six months to allow the bones to mend would have lain ahead; this spell would be followed by a painful period to restore movement to long immobile and stiffened joints and then muscle-rebuilding therapy. However, at Pegasus after the surgeons had straightened his bones, replacing where necessary with synthetic material, his legs were immediately encased in pulsating splints. These stimulated the blood supply to the damaged sections of his lower limbs; together with the judicious addition of bone regenerating medication and a careful manipulation of his blood composition meant that Buzz was already onto light exercises.

He told me, "I was careful not to lose any big pieces from my legs, so it's only a matter of sticking the bits together and the Docs say that I should be back in action in less than two weeks' time. Then I want to analyse that sample I found just before the mountain fell onto us."

After a slight pause, when for once Buzz appeared to be at a loss for words, he said hesitantly, "I suppose Juanita has come to terms with Sunny's death by now. I need to speak with her; she's never been to see me, you know."

Buzz was referring to the death of his partner on that last fateful day of the earth tremor—the day that ended with his partner crushed to pulp in the ruins of their transporter.

The big black man turned his bearded face to look straight into my eyes, then said sombrely, "What will you do about Pat's outburst in the control centre?"

I guessed that some kind friend, (for whatever reason), had told Buzz of his wife's distressed outpouring of disparagement and invective while she was waiting for information of the missing exploration team.

I placed a hand on the big man's shoulder and smiled. "I don't know what you're talking about," I said, and passed on.

CHAPTER TWENTY

The extraordinary capabilities of the androids had a disquieting effect on me. First, there was the remarkable dance routine displayed by Anthea, followed by Paul's demonstration of phenomenal strength in saving the community from almost certain disaster. I determined that it was high time to see for myself just what the people responsible for these prodigies were doing. These were the same three men for whom I had gone to so much trouble to bring here from the other side of the world. These three scientists were to add one more variety to the disparate collection of people who had been assembled in this place. I had been curious to see how they worked, but first the general pressure of everyday routine, which was interrupted by the near explosion in the powerhouse and then the all-consuming effort to get the program back on course, had distracted me. Now I was determined to see what was happening in the isolated workshop which had been allocated for this purpose.

The team of technicians who designed and built androids operated in a quiet spacious laboratory away from all other activities. Theirs was the only undertaking on this entire floor; I thought once more that here was a part of the enterprise that I had never previously visited. I considered it a matter of principle that I personally visit everyone who was engaged in this bizarre enterprise and at least pretend to understand all that occurred within its confines. Now I found myself on a strange floor, approaching a section of my responsibilities of which I had almost no knowledge.

I wondered as I crossed the bare area to the Swiss scientist's laboratory if I had a psychological inhibition against visiting this particular department.

Later that day I was to remember this premonition and wonder once more if a sixth sense invariably found a more interesting problem to redirect my attention whenever the thought of coming here had entered my head. As I neared the door with the single appellation, "Robotics," a mellifluous contralto voice greeted me.

"Welcome, Mr Stern!"

The door swung open. I walked into a small reception area thinking, "They must employ a sophisticated system to recognise me so quickly." The door closed silently behind me. Then I remembered that I was wearing my identity tag— mystery solved!

There was seating here, but no other opening to the one through which I entered. I hesitated and looked around cautiously. I stood for a while looking about, then the wall directly in front slowly changed from a dark to a pale grey, then into a shimmering window of sparkling pinpoints of light. Through this curtain of luminosity I could make out three figures; they were standing motionless with arms folded; I wondered how long they had been watching me. They wore the latest fashion in Pegasus clothing, the all-in-ones, the single piece close fitting body stockings, which were manufactured on base. The only variant between them was the differing shades of blue.

As was normal for men at Pegasus, all were completely bald. They were all slim, the most notable difference being in height. The baldness was the result of a hormone pill, which had become popular and was freely available; it had first come into common use to enable males to dispense with the necessity of shaving which most men found irksome. Then when baldness eventually followed, this in itself set a new fashion—a fashion that gradually evolved into covering the head on special occasions with elaborately styled and gaudily coloured headdress. From the community point of view, the hormone decreased male aggressiveness, which was a decided benefit in the restricted close-contact environment such as life in Pegasus entailed.

Curt, the tallest, smiled carefully and said, "We thought that you had forgotten about us Ro, but now that you're here we will try to make your visit interesting!"

I felt at a disadvantage and immediately set about trying to redress matters by enthusing over the part played by robot Paul, in the powerhouse drama.

"We are all in your debt; to your robot and his action in cutting off the fuel supply to the reactor," and added, "I'm sorry that Paul was destroyed."

The three slim men made no comment for several seconds and as I was beginning to wonder whether I had said the wrong thing, Curt answered in his cold clinical voice, "D.O.X.5 merely did what was expected; the task was well within the range of his capability. Would you care to see how far we have progressed with his replacement?" I cautiously passed through the shimmering wall of light to follow the three men.

"I think that the logical place to begin will be the

classrooms." Curt led the way towards a seemingly blank wall which, on receiving a signal from a ring on Curt's casually waved hand, immediately shimmered into an opalescent door-shaped opening. I was particularly interested to notice that the final shape was tapered slightly inwards toward the top of the opening, matching the ancient Aztec style of doorway. I wondered if there was any significance in this. I made a mental note to examine the library for details of what was known of Aztec culture; there may be a clue there to indicate how these three unusual people thought. I was acutely conscious that I knew less about the attitudes and philosophy of the three Swiss than any other group within the community. I had developed an uneasy feeling of distrust of these people, a feeling that I could not account for in any rational manner but was bound to consider the fearful hazard to the whole enterprise if these three ever took it into their heads to dominate the new culture that was envisaged! If they ever decided that they were dissatisfied with the organisation of the new world, thirty to forty super-strong Androids under direct control of the scientists who had created them could easily ensure complete domination.

A sobering thought.

We entered a room decorated throughout in shades of yellow.

"We colour our classrooms in accordance to the level of ability of the students," said Curt. The entire floor area was occupied with a toy train layout; admittedly this was the largest layout that I had ever seen, but a train set!

Seated at the six desks that were set around the layout, were four men and two women.

"How on earth does an over-grown train set fit into Robotics?" I asked incredulously.

"We use this method to instil multi-directional thinking," replied Curt. "This group is our most recent intake; they have only been with us for twenty days and they are restricted to the two inner tracks; there are two more to contend with before they move on."

At that very moment a thin faced man with a sallow complexion and slanting, dark eyes let out a terrifying yell; he banged his clenched fists down noisily and repeatedly on the desk in front of him and then ran from the room.

Curt lifted his pale eyebrows for a minute, then in an indifferent voice drawled, "Someone who can't stand the pace."

I watched in fascination as the five remaining contrasting coloured trains circled round, criss-crossing among the interweaving tracks.

"But what is the objective of it all?" I queried.

"You'll notice that there are no signals," said Curt. "The objective is to be first to complete ten circuits; of course each person is trying to do the same; the only rule is that the train approaching from the right has priority."

At that moment two trains collided; a hooter sounded and one of the men, looking sheepish, left his desk to reset the train that was derailed.

"Give us a demonstration Paul," he pleaded.

Paul went over to the young man's controls, flicked over the first and second controller and immediately commenced to operate the two red trains around the full layout; the other trains joined in. The different coloured trains flashed all over the tracks; as each engine completed a circuit a light registered on that person's control console. I was bewildered. I had difficulty following the rapid movement that was taking place; the most notable feature was that the red trains were constantly moving, often at frightening speed; as an opposing train crossed in front of them they would pause, then almost as the last carriage of the other train cleared the track the red engine seemed to scrape the end and then raced away to complete another circuit. As there were five crossings to each track on every circuit, the effort required to note the positions of all the other trains at varying stages and to calculate their different speeds, I considered impossible; but Paul quickly notched up ten full circuits before handing over the controls to an admiring figure whose place he had occupied.

"They can only practice for one hour at a time," commented Curt, "then they have to relax; but once they have mastered the necessary technique they are ready for the next class which is really difficult." He led the way to an adjoining room.

This room was decorated in blue; here six more students were controlling the flight of miniature aeroplanes! The small models were contained within a fine mesh material that formed a five-meter cube.

Again Curt offered an introduction to what was taking place.

"The objective is to control the plane from take-off; it then climbs to maximum height, completes two circuits and spirals down to land again. In this case however the six planes have to take off at closer and closer intervals and then alternate flights are in contrary directions. The models are electrically powered and each controller is responsible for transmitting varying power levels to control the speed as well as navigating." The brightly coloured models were dashing round and round inside the cage; occasionally one would land, a brief pause, then an indicator light on the appropriate desk would increase the counter by one more digit; then off again to join the other flying aircraft. My head was spinning as I tried to keep track of the different coloured planes; I couldn't concentrate on the question I wished to put; eventually I turned my back to the show, then after a pause exclaimed, "But what is the point of all this?"

Curt answered with a question, "Did you notice the altered features on each model as it landed?"

I said, "It took all my attention to count the number of times each one touched down, let alone any other details." Curt nodded. "Each controller is able to alter up to five distinguishing features on his own model; it is up to his opponents to spot which ones they are; the whole purpose of our training is to encourage our students to open their minds to alternative possibilities, to anticipate the unexpected and then exploit it. We have found that traditional teaching methods trap ways of thinking into rigid patterns of trying to remember established details. Facts which are easily available in any library. Fossilise the natural freedom of the brain to look at every new fact at face value. We are reversing the process, opening the mind to look for unusual events and wonder why. The future of our work lies in far greater development of the Psycherak brain, and these are the only people who will be able to do it. The existing Androids represent the limit of our own capability. To improve on our work we need fresh young minds unrestricted by existing conventions; minds that are free from rigid lines like those railway tracks, minds that are prepared for the unusual and the novel, can grab hold of it, extract the novelty and use it."

I noted the passion and enthusiasm of the zealot in Curt's

excited voice and burning eyes; I once more wondered about the aspirations of these people.

"We are quite determined to convert Anthea into a qualified flight-manager who will be competent to guard us against unforeseen conditions during our journey through space."

"How many students are you teaching?" I interrupted.

"Eighteen," replied Curt, "they are in groups of six, which enables each of us to concentrate on just two students at any one period; you will realise that there is a thirty-day interval between groups and that they work largely by themselves. Now we will look in on the senior group; an all-female group interestingly."

In stark contrast to the previous rooms, the next one was almost entirely black. Apart from the dull coloration this room was more in keeping with a traditional laboratory with normal workbenches supporting recognisable scientific apparatus.

Herman took up the narrative. "Our activities here are mainly exploring new, and by that we mean faster ways of storing and retrieving information."

He continued, "The reason for this room being blacked out like this is because we work largely with light in one form or another and any extraneous source or reflection could cause confusion. Our present interest revolves around 'Halo bacterium Halobium'; we have extracted the pigment from these bugs to provide the basis for short-term computer memory or RAMs. The pigment is in fact a miniature solar cell and by cooling this with liquid nitrogen to slow the reaction time to a speed that we can handle, we can switch the cells on with red light and off with green. Dr Lette Birger has made thin films of the pigment suspended in membranes like those, which surround living cells and encased them in plastic. A Helium-neon laser directs a spot of green or red light onto the film, flipping different groups of molecules into the red or green state. A scanner moves the laser over the film, storing memories as a mosaic of molecular traffic lights; of course reading them is rather trickier. These memories are surprisingly compact; a thin film two centimetres wide will store 200 million bits. The design of speedier memories is vital if ever we are to construct electronic brains that will not only compare with, but exceed the human model which is our present target."

I said nothing!

Curt then suggested that we move on to the more physical side of their work. We passed through another doorway into a spacious white clinical accommodation; the area was divided into cubicles. Some had their curtains closed.

"This whole lab is remarkably like a hospital," I commented.

"Of course we are in a related field," replied Curt with a supercilious smirk. He opened the curtain to a cubicle and stood aside to allow me to precede him. Laid out on an adjustable height operating table was a skeleton! That was my immediate conclusion. However, as Paul started to explain his particular problems and how he dealt with them, I could see that there were many differences between what was on the operating table and a normal human skeleton. Paul, who was never heard to speak to anyone other than the other two, was, even more than his two companions, an unknown quantity to me; now, as he gradually warmed to his own speciality, his high-pitched voice began to sparkle with enthusiasm and vigour.

"It took years of trial and error to find the perfect blend of strength and flexibility that could also be formed to the shape we required. We copied the human skeleton for obvious reasons; we intended making a replica of a human. We also decided to copy the design of the major joints. Because our skeletal material is both stronger and lighter than bone, however, we can eliminate many of the smaller joints; we just use a thinner replica bone and allow it to flex up or down. It is similar to a combination of bone and cartilage; you could call it synchondrosic, because we also attain excellent axial movement. We achieve greater rotation of the spine than a human could possibly manage and, you will note, without segmentation!"

I realised that this would explain the altogether extraordinary movements which Anthea displayed during her dance routine.

"I see there's no skull."

"Not necessary," said Paul. "These figures don't require jawbones to eat; remember, jaws were originally intended to tear and bite tough food such as raw flesh. Neither do we need to protect the brain; our brain is located within the chest cavity. We cause the lips to move to simulate speech, but that is purely cosmetic. We make the heads completely from synthesised skin supported as necessary with silicone stiffening and padding. Right, now we'll have a look at the head of Paul number two!"

We all moved towards a cubicle enclosed with a transparent material instead of a curtain. Inside were two pigs!

I gazed in amazement, as well I might; I thought I knew what was going on in Pegasus; but I was totally unaware that it contained any living creatures other than human.

It was my own fault; I'd never taken the trouble to see what was happening here before today.

"What on earth are pigs doing here?" I demanded.

"You're looking at our synthetic skin production unit."

I was incredulous. "Are you saying that you use pig skin for those Androids?"

"That's exactly what I'm saying."

"But why live animals? Growing skin in a culture medium independent of the body is common practice, so where do animals like pigs fit in?"

Paul patiently explained. "It may be a common practice, but do you know what the limitations are? After a 50% increase in area, the system breaks down and we have not as yet found out why."

"But why pigs?" I protested.

"Because human skin is not tough enough. You must remember that human skin is constantly being renewed. Our Androids need a skin that will last a lifetime, whatever length of time that may be. Let me explain.

"For simple straight pieces we take a sheet of epidermis from the pig's belly; we can grow that in culture for about a month to increase overall dimension and quality. This can then be formed into legs or arms or chest. Of course it has to be prepared first."

"You mean tanned?"

"Of course, but we prefer to describe the process as perpetuating. It will always require regular feeding with a suitable emulsified oil, but with care it will last virtually forever."

Paul continued, "But then we come to the tricky bits, like ears and faces; for these we use a pattern or mould and encourage the skin to grow over it and because of the difficult shapes we need a constant and abundant supply of nutrients, hence the live animals."

"I still don't understand," I said, feeling foolish. I couldn't see the connection.

"Watch," said Paul. "Those animals don't realise that we are here; this partition has one way light transmission at present." He pressed a button and the partition twinkled; the pigs immediately looked at the four people watching them, then just as quickly walked over to investigate.

"Pigs are curious animals, you know," smiled Paul.

But my eyes were riveted onto the pig's sides, which had been turned away, until they decided to come to see who was looking at them.

"What is that growth underneath?" I exclaimed.

Paul laughed. "It depends on which one you're looking at. The one nearest to you is my new face; the other is a test penis; not a copy of mine I hasten to assure you. Our next model is going to be a complete man."

I was almost speechless as Paul continued, "Those special features are actually a living part of the animal and they will continue to develop until we decide that they are ripe; then we will remove them—it's a very simple operation. The animals are under no distress, I assure you. We actually start them in that particular position quite deliberately; the pig thinks of them as youngsters suckling and is agitated for a day or two when they are gone. We will need at least two pigs to transfer to our new home when we go, so that we can commence production of androids at an early date. I'm assuming that you accept the advantages they offer us?"

"Oh, yes, of...of course," I stammered, "but you've given me quite a surprise. I would never dream that the androids I've seen were covered in pig skin!"

The three Swiss smiled at each other. They were obviously

pleased with themselves; our whole group moved to another cubicle where Anthea was standing in one corner.

"I think that Ro Stern still needs convincing," murmured Curt to his companions. "Anthea, remove your clothes and lie on the table.

"Now we've explained how we make it, just have a good feel at R.101 here and judge the results for yourself."

He lightly ran his hand over the beautifully shaped legs and belly of Anthea's body. The skin colour was a delicate shade of coffee touched with bronze; the lighting in the room added a warm sheen. As I followed Curt's example, I thought how the skin felt like satin with a thistledown covering of fine hair, similar in nature to the head of a very young baby; altogether exquisite!

I was reluctant to remove my hand, such was the sensual pleasure I experienced; I would have continued but then I became aware that the other three were watching my face in amusement. I snatched my hand away.

"The third basic component of our work is synthetic muscle; Herman spent years searching for a suitable combination of elements which could be polymerised to give the properties we require."

"And what was that?"

"The property to contract when stimulated with an electrical current; again a copy of animal life but yet again, a substance that would remain stable without a blood supply to nourish it. Let me show you."

Curt placed both his hands on Anthea's thigh; feeling very carefully, he pressed hard with one thumb; then with the nails of his other hand slowly tore the side of her thigh open. The skin separated with a sucking, slithering sound of tearing that made me gulp; I had witnessed several serious injuries in my lifetime and thought that I had a fairly strong stomach, but this clinical dissection of a beautiful figure struck a sensitive chord inside my brain.

And when Curt went on to say, "Let me get a battery and I'll show you what occurs when I stimulate the two opposing muscles," I hurriedly said, "Not just now. I'm afraid that I have a meeting with Pete Morgan at twelve." I virtually fled from the lab!

Curt called after me, "Next time you come I'll show you how we tweak the Psychiatric Brain, and to get it to make the music you heard Anthea dance to."

In the privacy of our own apartment that evening, while narrating my experience of the morning to Beth. I said, "I've never appreciated how clinically austere a specialist can become. I expect it has much to do with habit and when all is said and done, there are no feelings or senses involved, an android is a machine; but without question my stomach heaved when he ripped open that leg." I was pacing up and down our comfortable private lounge, an indication of my perplexity with the enigmatic robot designers.

"There's another facet to the story. Paul told me that after trials they found that injecting the figures with silicone produced too firm a texture. Where joints caused the skin to bend, unnatural looking folds and cracks formed. They side-stepped this problem by filling the figures with chips of the same material; however, to achieve an authentic appearance and feel, they now inflate a porous layer immediately below the skin with air!"

"So the marvellous figure, which Anthea displayed in her dance routine, was largely due to compressed air?" questioned a smiling Beth.

"Absolutely, but here's the clincher. Curt solemnly suggested that the technique is transferable to humans. It would be quite possible to eliminate all visible signs of ageing! All that would be required is a little subsurface surgery, to introduce microscopic tubing, a miniature cylinder of compressed gas with a pressure governor and he would guarantee to make wrinkled faces and sagging breasts a thing of the past!"

"Well, if I find you spending more time with Anthea, I'll know the reason why," laughed Beth, "but I can assure you, I'm not going to inflate my boobs! You will have to put up with things the way they are at present."

I could finally smile and, approaching Beth, placed both hands on her shoulders and whispered, "I'm quite satisfied with the existing arrangements." Then I remembered something else.

"They also told me that they proposed to change the pressurising medium to an inert gas; they feel embarrassed that Robot D.O.X.5 burnt as quickly as he did."

CHAPTER TWENTY ONE

Ben paid a rare visit to my office one morning; he immediately opened the conversation with a surprising statement:

"The prototype will be ready for final pre-commissioning checks tomorrow, Ro. We've made better progress than I expected and so I propose to commence flight testing. If we restrict the height to 500 metres we should avoid showing the world what we've been doing for the last five years."

A thrill of suppressed excitement ran through my entire being; this was the moment that we had been anticipating and working toward for so many years.

Ben continued, "I think it prudent to conduct the early assessment in full daylight, but if all goes well with no unforeseen problems, the real evaluation test flight must take off under cover of darkness. We've no way of calculating the rate of ascent and we are particularly concerned to know if it will vary when we start to leave the earth's gravitational field. Then I would like your views on the duration of the flight, as we have already agreed this will be restricted to one only in order to maintain whatever secrecy we still enjoy. If we were to run any more we might find we have enemy rockets waiting for us on our return. We must assume that Devlin Bhutto made a clean getaway and reported to his masters. Pete Morgan says that he has no report from Chino Security to the contrary and so we've decided that means the death ray protective screen must be compromised. It can only be a matter of time before an organisation that employs clever people like Bhutto works out the formula." We both looked grim as the implication in this statement forced its potential hazards into our thoughts.

Then Ben continued, "The general consensus of opinion supports a flight in the direction of K34. Of approximately two hundred and eighty hours. This will enable us to calibrate our instrumentation and should provide sufficient operational experience of the Sansung converter to give the designers the data they need to produce the blueprints for the full-scale version. The youngsters are confidently expecting to be able to increase the velocity to a figure in excess of 90% of light speed, but without a test-flight Professor Sansung refuses to speculate on what may happen. Personally I need a tremendous quantity of basic data to enable the computer analysts to compile a programme of control for the anti-grav apparatus; so I suggest that we return by way of Mars; the gravitational differential from Earth should allow us to calculate the different values we require. Then all we need is a table to accommodate variations from earth's norm. The parameters within which we must work immediately have been decided as being from minus 10% to plus 500%. Now, can we review the crewing schedule?"

Ben continued, "I would like to add Kratsky to the list which we last discussed; there is so much unproven circuitry that a person with his ability could prove invaluable in case of difficulties; I'm assuming that we can live together for the few days that we expect to be away."

I smiled at the last remark. Kratsky was not a very popular

person. We remained engrossed in discussion for another hour before I said, "That's everything as far as I can see; now show me this wonderful contraption that's going to change all our futures, including the history of Earth. The last I saw was the production of sections before any assembly took place."

"It's not only our future that's going to be changed," commented Ben grimly. "The most powerful organisation on Earth won't be able to keep what we've achieved quiet. I'm only sorry that I won't be here to see how the world reacts when the full story comes out." We headed for the elevator, which took us down to ground level; here we transferred to another that descended into the very bowels of the rock, which lay beneath the desert surface. The journey took us through five metres of the thick foundations of Pegasus. The concrete-lined shaft continued downwards for several minutes.

"I'd no idea that it was so deep," I said.

Ben replied, "Mac told me that it was necessary to continue until they came to a solid rock strata without faults through which to tunnel; we head due south for three kilometres to reach the assembly site."

At the foot of the lift shaft Ben and I walked a few paces to the Magalev passenger car that was waiting. The Magalev was the basis of all surface transport on earth at this time. It operated on magnetic principles, so this transport system was a variation of the anti-grav effect. There was no need for wheels—the transporter depended on magnetism to remove friction and a linear motor to provide movement. The car carried us smoothly and silently along a wide brightly illuminated passage hewn from a purple coloured crystalline rock. Lighting came from two continuous tubes that had been clipped to each side of the tunnel roof. The light sparkled on the larger red and blue individual crystals that were liberally distributed throughout the length of the tunnel. "You can see where the latest costume jewellery originates," laughed Ben as he noticed the direction of my gaze attracted to the dazzling show. At the end of the brief ride we left the car for a moving staircase. "We're not so far from the surface here." We were now inside a circular chamber formed from cast aluminium panels. "Terminus," said Ben, "we'll take a look at the exterior first so that you'll have some idea of the overall appearance; there's helmets on the racks." We donned the bulky helmets which completely surrounded our skulls. "Not very convenient, but at least we won't have to wear them for long and the death ray certainly keeps us free from visitors at present. Pete tells me that our Chinese guards still collect bodies from the surrounding area from time to time." The exit from the terminal brought us just to the edge of a gleaming giant saucer and it was here that I had my first view of the prototype spacecraft.

"We'll take a car to show you the full picture."

We entered an anti-grav vehicle and slowly circled this creation of man's ingenuity. This entity was the result of the most advanced and ambitious scheme ever envisaged, and was about to cause a tremendous furore throughout the world.

I had been present at the many meetings held to decide the final design of the spaceship; I had seen the blueprints, the computerised graphics and also sketches by one of the engineers with some artistic talent; but now as I looked down on the vitrified surface of this grey monster, I was subjected to an intense thrill of wonderment; a sense of anticipation which sent a chill of apprehension chasing up and down my spine.

I was looking at the result of five years of frustration,

anxiety, tears and toil; not a few deaths could also be attributed to this creation. I realised that I had left out the laughs and happy occasions, which had also been part of this period; but my overall mood was sombre.

Gazing down on this product of so much effort and hope finally satisfied me that our plans and dreams would really succeed; the occasions when deep black despair had almost overcome my outward calm were forgotten. However, not forgotten were the times when I doubted that I would ever see this day!

As the drawings had predicted, the ship was just like two thick saucers arranged face to face; where the top and bottom were joined together there was left a flat vertical band one metre wide which circled the ship. In the inverted position that I was looking at now, the raised ring which formed the base on which a saucer would rest, became the collecting aperture to the Sansung particle drive—the man-made motive system that was to carry the voyagers to far-distant worlds. There were no portholes of course; all information of exterior conditions would be gathered by antennae enclosed within the ship's protective Corundum diamond hard glossy grey shielding and displayed on the dials and screens of the consoles inside.

I gazed at this wonder in silence; my thoughts drifted back along the episodes that had led to this day; I remembered a holiday on the lonely island in the barrier reef where this dream had started. I remembered the feelings of dread when I had been told of the explosives, which had been carried inside a man's body. I thought of the time when I had been literally snatched from the sea by the giant cargo plane and I also remembered the indifferent expression on Curt's face as he slammed shut the door of the power house after witnessing the fate of a robot. Not a man, admittedly, but it had the form and shape of a human being. Also of the time with Hank as we both struggled desperately to cut holes in the powerhouse roof. All these events had led to this moment; this moment of wonder must be the climax of my life. Surely nothing would ever surpass this pinnacle of fulfilment.

With a jerk of my head I spoke to Ben who had remained silent to allow his leader the privilege of contemplation.

"Okay Ben, let's look inside."

Ben returned our car to the park immediately adjacent to the entrance of the terminal building. Once inside we could remove the cumbersome helmets and move more freely. Ben now led the way to the entrance of the spaceship; this was situated beneath the craft. He went on to explain,

"We decided to make the opening halfway to the perimeter in case we have to land on a soft surface; if the weight of the ship causes us to sink below the surface we will not have so far to dig ourselves out; at the same time we retain some protection from not being immediately exposed to outside conditions." He allowed me to precede him up the short flight of steps that led into the spaceship.

Inside, several people were conscientiously working from circuit diagrams, calling to each other softly as they re-checked every piece of equipment for the umpteenth time. I was dismayed by the makeshift appearance in evidence in all that I saw; this didn't look as if it could go anywhere, let alone space flight.

"We have left everything easily accessible Ro, in case we need to get at it in a hurry; you will notice that the essential functional controls are few and well within reach of one person. this will be a simple ship to fly; the most difficult task will be to determine the attractive field strength of whatever gravitational field we allow ourselves to enter."

The interior of the ship was three meters high in the centre, falling away from the almost flat central section and curved together towards the edges. The bold columns that formed the force field that would convert the Hydrogen of space into the energy that would propel the ship indefinitely occupied the centre of the ship. The control modules were set around this central ring. Towards the sides of the cabin were eight bunks. "There won't be much privacy in here I'm afraid," said Ben grinning. Privately he wondered how difficult it would be to live in such close proximity to Kratsky, a prospect he did not relish.

The preliminary to the test-flight proper was conducted the following day. Without incident the giant saucer rose slowly and almost imperceptibly into the clear blue sky. It attained the programmed 500 metres above the barren desert amid wild whoops of excitement and relief from those most intimately concerned with the construction of the ship and returned somewhat later than was strictly necessary, back to earth.

Once down, the news of the successful test which had taken place and which had not been made general knowledge, spread like wildfire. There was an immediate clamour to be allowed onto the test flight the following day. Many and varied were the reasons advanced by the eager specialists needing to test his or her particular theory in the unknown conditions of space. Sadly, all realised that there would be no other opportunity; when the final version was ready, it was to be a once only journey; this was the only evaluation flight which would be required to prove once and for all time that the principles were sound.

CHAPTER TWENTY ONE

It was to be the only time when I had need of my supreme final authority!

I accepted the value of the passionate arguments in support of the many schemes, which were put to me; but I never lost sight for one second of the cardinal duty for which I was responsible; my prime objective was to lead an expedition to another planet!

Fortunately for the ultimate success of the venture I had the strength of mind never to waver from this paramount principle. So, however sincere and rational the reason in favour of allowing one extra person to benefit from an additional place on the test flight, to do this would have accepted, be it ever so limited, a possible risk for delay towards the primary goal. I was determined that nothing, but nothing, should be allowed to do that!

The duty officer who was on duty by a rota, which had been arranged many months previously, was the only occupant of the entire concrete dome when the time for the test flight approached. Every other soul, whether support-group or colonist, in sick bay or otherwise supposedly engaged in essential activity, bore witness to the seemingly impossible ease with which the test flight of the first true flying saucer was achieved. No sound was to be heard from the gigantic shape that slowly eased off the barren desert sand and floated upwards into the lonely, dark and gloomy sky; there was no moon, no starlight to allow vision beyond the limited distance of perhaps a hundred metres; then the looming disc vanished into the glowering clouds. A subdued, thoughtful audience returned indoors to contemplate our future.

CHAPTER TWENTY TWO

———◆———

The ultimate design of the Spaceship, which was to carry the venturers, had been decided upon, and large parts had been under construction for many months before the prototype made its demonstration flight. The anti-grav principle was well proven by now; one of the few missing pieces of the mosaic which remained to be added was detailed performance results from within differing gravitational fields. Also required was operational data for the Sansung Particle Drive; theoretical calculations were fine up to a point, but the technically qualified members among the venturers wished for empirical results before they abandoned the known facts of this world and finally and irrevocably cast their lot into such an unproved proposition.

There was an insistent demand for confirmation of the theories and suppositions that had been made and the prototype was expected to satisfy these concerns.

The prototype did not qualify for a name—it was merely a test bed; but the vessel, which was to carry so many hopes and expectations to an entirely new world, must have a name. Many and varied were the suggestions put forward, but after lengthy debate, *Han Venturer* was finally accepted by all.

This name was meant to convey appreciation to the country and especially that country's leader whose unstinting support alone had made the adventure possible.

Now, immediately after the launch of the first working model, assembly of the real thing was commenced; large sections had been formed inside the workshop, but there was a limit to the size, which could be handled. This vessel would be 250 metres in diameter. For practical purposes this meant that sections, which were 33 metres wide by 100 metres long, were considered to be the maximum size for safe transportation to the final assembly site, which was out in the bleak desert at the end of the underground tunnel. Hank was excitedly explaining to Annette how this was done. Annette was not really interested; her own work provided enough problems to fully occupy her mind, but she was sufficiently concerned about all our futures to realise that these mechanical events were important.

"We install the anti-grav giros into each section as they are built up; then we start them up just prior to moving the section out to the final assembly station. You should hear the roar when we start injecting the compressed air to set them spinning! It's like being out on the runway when the intercontinental jets take off."

"I suppose that you have ear protection," interjected Annette severely.

"Of course, but you can feel the sound through your feet; the entire building vibrates; do you know that it takes 24hrs with the compressors running flat out to build up a sufficient pressure of air in the storage bottles to get one gyro running at anything like enough revs? Once one of the gyros exceeded the standard speed and developed too much lift; the whole section shot up to the roof of the workshop," Hank laughed. "You should have seen Ben Hoyt—he was dancing around like a madman."

CHAPTER TWENTY TWO

"How did you recover that?" asked a suddenly interested Annette.

"Oh, I climbed up a rope and then Ben told me how to release the vacuum of the casing; this allows air to enter and that soon slows the gyro; I came down with a bit of a bump, but nothing serious. That stuff that the ship is made with is like cast iron now and it still has to have a really tough finishing coat on top of that." Hank bubbled on: "When we have all the rotors run up to full speed we fit temporary controls to enable us to float the segments out to the assembly site. You should see the size that it's going to be—it's nearly as big as Pegasus!"

"How much have you put together?" asked Annette.

"Just over half but that's what I've come to tell you about; I'll have to work tonight. It seems that the whole project is under pressure to complete everything as fast as possible!"

Even now ultimate success was not guaranteed. At one of the regular meetings, which took place to keep all Pegasus personnel informed of events that were pertinent, I opened the proceedings with a grim statement.

"We have been advised directly from the Imperial Palace that unprecedented efforts are being made against the Chinese government to force into the open, and I quote: 'The sinister experiments at present being undertaken in the heart of China. There is a concerted and determined vocal and media instigated campaign, attacking the leadership of China.'"

This statement caused a great deal of unease among the venturers; surely we hadn't come all this way, suffered from fear and apprehension, worked long and hard, mainly uncomplainingly, then forced our minds to contemplate a speculative future for it all to come to nothing?

Some of these attacks could be witnessed on the T.V. programmes which were picked up and relayed on the Pegasus network. What were not seen were the inter-governmental pressure, the dealing and bargaining that went on between all governments. Of course, any one country could not easily kick China around, but it was still susceptible to combined pressure when several countries banded together, and this was happening now! Ho Chek had his spies working overtime trying to discover what inducements were on offer to entice so many differing countries to join forces against him. What he had failed to realise was that the anger came not from any particular government, but from one obsessed criminal mind. For it was necessarily a personal attack on Ho Chek; he had an amused contempt for his own politicians; all the support for project Pegasus came as a result of instructions issued directly from the Palace. Democratic institutions meant little to Ho Chek, the man who had fought his way to the top of the largest country on Earth. Fortunately for the venturers at Pegasus, Ho Chek was as equally determined as Dr Olletti.

Privately, I asked Teng Ho for his assessment of the situation and the prospects of continuing support from our patron?

Teng smiled grimly. "I'm confident that we have nothing to fear in the immediate future. Opposition to Ho Chek will merely make him more determined to continue with his own plans. We need only worry if someone can offer a greater opportunity to fame! At this stage I can't see anything creating a bigger sensation than Space Flight.

Of course if there is ever any question of us not pulling it off, he would throw us to the wolves in a flash. I keep him informed of our progress, but without doubt he will have at least one other informant inside our party."

Pete interrupted at this juncture to add, "I've received unconfirmed stories of a crack force of mercenary storm troopers being recruited. I have no definite information of the theatre of operations, but since drugs were legalised, brothels are commonplace, there's precious little else to fight over. Gambling and entertainment cities are all that make any real profit these days and they have been organised by the major criminal syndicates for so long that it's difficult to imagine a gangland war breaking out over territory now. I'm left with the distinct impression that we are the target. If the Bhutto's got clean away with the information that was available around the base at that time, it is not impossible to credit him with discovering the basis of the death ray and the protective element in the helmets; especially if that rumour about Sino Research being a front for one of the major crime syndicates has any truth to it."

Ched broke in: "Are you seriously supposing that we may be subject to a direct physical assault on Pegasus?"

"Since you've put into words what is at the back of my mind, the answer is yes!" Pete continued, "And I'm sure the next thing you'll say is that we still have the Chinese army guarding us; well, for your enlightenment, our military protection consists of one company. They have to patrol the perimeter of the area covered by the cone of radiation from the satellite. This is approximately a 10-kilometre radius around Pegasus; this means a border of 70 kilometres, for 24 hours each day and for this there are not many more than one hundred men. As long as the secret of the death ray remained restricted, that proved an effective protection; but now it would be unrealistic to depend only on that! I can assure you from bitter experience, very few people are immune from bribery or coercion; just think of our own experience here. There is no place on Earth that is secure from a determined effort to break into, given sufficient time and resources."

I said, "I suggest that we spend some time considering what the primary target may be, and the type of weaponry which may be deployed against us. Then, as a preliminary exercise in how to deal with something we don't like, as our constitution lays down, what we are to do to counter this potential development. I also suggest that we institute maximum effort to complete our vessel quickly, to enable us to leave this corrupted planet as soon as possible. Is it feasible to organise three shifts working, Ched?"

As Ched nodded his agreement, I concluded, "I'm sure we all have enough to think about for tonight so I'll close the meeting."

CHAPTER
TWENTY THREE

The flight of the prototype spaceship had been noted by both official observatories and many amateur star gazers. These were quick to note and record their sightings and speculate on what manner of object it was that they had witnessed leaving the Earth's atmosphere. This in turn aroused a fury of speculation; the approximate area from which the object had appeared was easily calculated as being in the Sinkian area of China and probably the Taklimakan desert; this led to renewed demands for more information.

China no longer denied every story or speculated theory, but simply refused to make any form of comment. This autocratic attitude drove the news seekers wild with anger! All this attention and display of anger was regularly witnessed on the T.V. screens inside Pegasus and, after my warning about the additional pressure being applied against China, further fuelled the anxiety of the personnel.

The return of the test-bed model was scheduled to land under cover of darkness; there was no fixed time; this had been left to the discretion of the crew to decide. Twenty-five days after leaving a signal was received to inform the communications officer that the prototype was within landing range. This news spread throughout the base rapidly; a crowd quickly gathered around the control desk waiting for additional information.

The excited chatter was stilled as Ben's voice came over the lasercom.

"Please get Ro Stern to the desk." Reception was perfect and everyone could detect the anxious tone in Ben's voice.

I acknowledged immediately, "What is it Ben?"

"We were searching for the landing area on broad scan, Ro. We soon located the beacon on top of Pegasus but then we noticed several moving objects converging towards you; we weren't expecting to see any signs of life or activity within a radius of 500 km, so we switched to high definition mode."

A pause, followed by, "It looks as though you are about to receive visitors; are you expecting anyone?"

I looked at Pete and then Ched; thought for a moment and then said, "How quickly could you descend to ground level Ben?"

Ben's reply came at once: "We're at ten thousand metres, just beyond normal eyesight; we could be down to thirty metres in two minutes. It would take longer to actually touch down to terra-firma. I suggest that we wait here and report movements to you; we can resolve detail down to five centimetres on our infrared intensifiers. How do you feel about us finding out what effect the anti-meteorite laser screens have?"

"We must have positive proof that their intentions are aggressive," I snapped. "Just observe for the moment."

I looked over to where an apprehensive Oval was listening. "Can you mount scanners on the top of Pegasus, Oval? We'll need as much detailed information as we can get. I have a plan, but we must be careful with the timing." I looked around once more; my eyes fell upon Hank and stopped there. "In case my plan is not successful we must barricade ourselves in until the Chinese military send reinforcements; will you gather a team together to close the access to the ship? Then get under cover at terminus and barricade the doors from the inside."

Hank quickly replied, "Leave it to me, Ro."

A tense twenty minutes followed; then Ben reported once more.

"There's ten heavy trucks, Ro. They are 3km away from you; now they have put on speed—they should reach Pegasus in about five minutes."

Exactly six minutes later a muffled explosion was heard; the building vibrated. Ben's anxious voice came over the air:

"Are you all right? We registered a violet shock wave from Pegasus. Are you all right?"

I quickly replied, "I'm not sure if we've suffered any casualties, but that was the proof I've been waiting for. Bring your ship down at once, Ben; when you are low enough, make a sweep across our Northern side; that's where they seem to be attacking and as you pass over see what effect varying your gravitation field strength has; you remember what happened to you when you lifted the rock off Buzz's legs?"

Ben laughed out loud, "Do I! Here we come."

Shortly afterwards Oval's voice came over the internal intercom: "I'm watching trucks and men floating around and then dropping to the ground; two of the trucks dropped onto the building and exploded; the ones that hit the sand look as though they won't run again."

The waiting party round the control desk broke into laughs and shouts. "Well done Ro," they shouted.

I smiled in return, but replied in a sober voice: "Let's make sure there are no more before we celebrate."

Inside the aluminium walls of the terminal, at the desert end of the tunnel exit from Pegasus, Hank with two more young men of his own age were looking rather apprehensively at the makeshift barricade which they had hastily erected against the door that led out to the desert. The barricade consisted of one packing case of lighting equipment ready for installation in the spaceship; not very heavy, nor giving the group who had pushed it into position much confidence that it would stand up against a determined assault, but in the short space of time available that was all that they could find. They stood back by the side of the Magalev car wondering what else they could do. They didn't have long to wait; a violent explosion blasted the door and flimsy barricade into a cloud of dust and flying debris.

Hank gasped, "Let's get out of here." They stumbled into the car and slamming the drive lever over to the maximum, silently shot away along the tunnel; behind them they heard shouts of exultation as the attackers burst into the outer boundary of Pegasus.

During the journey along the tunnel Hank was thinking hard; he was ashamed of his failure to protect their home from invasion, but how could he have done more? He wondered desperately if he should have done better, but what? Whatever will Ro think of me? He felt sickened by the thought of having to face Annette with his disgrace. His mind was racing round and round: "How to prevent the intruders getting any further?"

The car in which they were travelling automatically slowed at the end of the journey in the station beneath the centre of Pegasus.

"I can't let them get into the main building," thought Hank; then an idea struck him; to one side of the area was a pile of heavy concrete sleepers left over from the construction of the perfectly level track which was essential for a Magalev line.

"Give me a hand!" he shouted to his companions; between them they carried two of these heavy sleepers to the car and after a struggle managed to place them across the car floor. By placing the sleepers not quite centrally they arranged for one end of each concrete block to protrude to almost touch each side of the tunnel.

"Now all we need is some opposition," grunted a grim Hank; with a terse expression on his face, he stood on the car with his hand on the control lever.

"I have a better idea!" shouted one of his companions. "Watch." He ran to the main circuit box which controlled all the electrics in the tunnel. Quickly opening the door he switched off one of the circuit breakers. "Now put the control over into the maximum position and when we see them coming we can switch on from here!" Hank immediately put the control on the car into position and stepped back from the battering ram that they had fashioned. All three men crouching low and restraining their laboured breathing hid themselves behind the rest of the spare sleepers to watch. They didn't have long to wait. A few moments later they saw a party of six men dressed in dark green battle dress and wearing light weight bullet proof jackets advancing cautiously along the tunnel; they trotted along, stooping low to keep their profile to a minimum. The tunnel ran perfectly straight so that the advancing troops were in sight for several minutes before Hank made his move. As he stepped out from behind his protective cover, shots immediately sang around his head;

he did not hesitate but threw over the contactor to the Magalev train. The train started moving forward slowly and silently, then quickly built up to full speed; it didn't have far to travel and caught the advancing soldiers completely by surprise. They were expecting return fire and failed to realise the significance of the rapidly advancing car coming towards them; it was soon too late to duck beneath the lethal battering ram that swept them to pulp like so many flies.

Two hours later I received a report from the leader of the reinforcements Brigadier Chien Lung. They had rushed out to the lonely site in the desert immediately on receipt of the urgent call for help from Pegasus. "We've covered the surrounding area thoroughly, Sir. I'm confident that there are no more outlaws."

"How did they pass our normal guards?" I asked.

The Officer replied, "I am responsible for your security here. I hold my position directly from the Imperial Palace. I apologise most sincerely for this intrusion. It would appear that because of the efficiency of the particle beam in keeping spies out our local commander has become lax in his responsibilities. He failed to notice that the captain of the guard had transferred all of this day's patrols to the southern sector. He was probably bribed to do this." The brigadier smiled grimly. "He didn't have long in which to enjoy his reward! I'm also confident that there will be no recurrence of this regrettable affair; I have ordered immediate increased protection; you have my word, it will not happen again."

As was my custom, I discussed the affair with Beth before retiring.

"The Chinese army troops cleared away all evidence of the attack before they left. I noticed particularly that there were no prisoners; we had the medics clear up the mess in the tunnel. Hank insisted on helping. He felt that he had let us down in allowing the attackers to get so far—he was looking distinctly green when I last saw him.   Ben came in cock-a-hoop. He knew the results of his little performance; it seems that the test flight was a complete success. He wanted to tell me what Mars is really like but I had to put him off. I didn't get a wink of sleep last night and I'm shattered."

CHAPTER
TWENTY FOUR

———◆———

Almost every inhabitant dwelling in Pegasus was present in the assembly hall. There were a few deliberate non-appearances; these were the ones who would not face the prospects of having to think more than they already did about their immediate future. For the rest, they tried to keep their deep down fear masked from each other. Most partners held hands; some, like Hank and Annette, unashamedly had their arms around each other; one or two of the younger men became noisily obstreperous.

When Professor Shasimoso who was a smiling, rotund, balding Japanese, began to speak there was instant silence; he began in his clinically piping voice:

"You will observe the thermal indicator; it shows that the temperature is within the permitted variance of plus or minus one degree of the ideal we expect to achieve, which is -59 degrees celsius."

A three-dimensional image projected onto the theatre's reproduction galvanic beam cascades showed a digital display of the temperature.

"Now we see the registration lights change from green to amber; this shows us that the programme is about to undergo a change; now the light is at red: this is to indicate that the defrost cycle has been initiated; this will occupy the next hour.

"We rejoin the process exactly fifty-five minutes later."

The three-dimensional image now showed a representation of an injection moulded casket two meters in length and wide enough and deep enough to accommodate a human body; the colour was light grey and was raised from the floor on two triangular supports.

"You will now notice that the frost has disappeared from the face plate; at this stage warm water is introduced throughout the main arteries and the lungs; this process will last for thirty seconds exactly; we find that the chilled body will withstand this degree of internal warming without trauma. Now the water inside the body is being replaced with heated synthetic blood, which is oxygen abundant; this will circulate for five minutes and then in its turn be replaced with the original blood from the subject. The next stage is dependent on the individual; the programme will wait until the neural responses indicate that they are in functional order. Experience shows this to vary; if you monitor the timer you will note that this subject required twelve minutes and thirty-five seconds. It is now time for the external water to drain away; the casket turns to an upright position and the subject steps out!

"As you will observe; I am the subject, here to demonstrate conclusively that the process is viable."

He paused. Ro thought that he was expecting applause.

There was a shuffling of feet, but no one seemed keen to start the questioning. Eventually Annette asked the Professor: "How long did the freezing process take?"

Professor Shasimoso hesitated. "It varies with the amount

of body fat on each subject, but our target is two minutes."

There were no more questions in public; people still preferred not to think too deeply about what lay in store for them.

Dr Stronberg however, together with his medical staff, would have the administrative responsibility of conducting the chilling process. They would be intimately involved with the mechanics of the freezing technique and therefore arranged to have a private discussion with Professor Shasimoso. He was more than willing to expound on his work, which had become his hobby as well. The professor had been disappointed that he had not had the opportunity to elucidate on what was for him a fascinating subject, so now he made up for it!

"We really must start several weeks ahead of the actual freezing," he said. "From studies completed over many years and on numerous animal subjects, we conclude that a carefully calculated diet that adds a degree of body fat ensures that the subjects have a readily available supply of nourishment to tide them over until the body re-establishes its normal functions when regeneration takes place. When we are dealing with humans I find it beneficial to induce them to take one of the tranquillisers. Venture press has been found suitable; followed by a simple injection to numb the area where we insert the catheter to withdraw blood. I'm sure I don't need to remind you, Dr Stronberg, that total withdrawal of blood from a body automatically lowers the body temperature and in so doing induces natural anaesthesia. The process then requires a rapid chilling of body tissue in mass. It is very important to avoid uneven chilling; this we achieve by flushing the entire system with a brine solution with a high percentage of Glycol and Formaldehyde; the temperature of this brine is -60 degrees c. and at this temperature works rapidly. You will recall how I stressed the need for a sterile environment in which the subjects are able to rid their systems of all earthly airborne impurities before we commence the chilling process; we have found that one hour suffices for this preparation; but the time delay has an adverse effect on the subjects' emotional condition; so we add a suitable narcotic into the air purification system, but now we present the operating staff with an additional problem; because of the narcotic in the atmosphere the porters must be different personnel to the chilling operatives, as they gradually become affected and their efficiency falls off..."

The conversation continued for some time and eventually Dr Stronberg was completely satisfied with the explanations he had been given and suitably impressed with the thought and attention to detail which had been demonstrated. "How did you become involved with such an unusual procedure?" he asked the Professor.

"I was with the Himalayan expedition of '33," was the reply. "Thor Johanson was leading; he had a particular objective in view; he had to return to base camp the previous season because of deteriorating weather but had noted the exact spot to return to with a radioactive beacon. (Whoops, forget that I said that, the natives are very touchy about what they call contaminating their mountains!) Thor had invited me because he knew of my interest in Cryobiology and at long last he was sure that he was onto something interesting. He was. But finding the creature was one thing; getting it out of a crevasse thirty metres below the surface was another. Thor had been determined to keep all knowledge of his speculation to the minimum number of people so we had a great deal of difficulty getting the shaggy bundle of mud and hair to the surface with minimum damage. I was actually with the party that went down into the chasm; we had taken crevasse ladders on the expedition and laid these across the opening, then lowered ourselves down. It took several hours to hack away the accumulation of ice and moraine that had fallen onto the creature over the centuries; but we eventually managed to fix a rope net around him and haul him to the surface; of course we did not know at that stage that the creature was male, but you can imagine the excitement when I stated that in my opinion this heap of mud and fur was animal and in a state of hibernation!

"If you remember, the creature has been rumoured to exist for decades; the so-called Yeti; it was eventually named after its discoverer, Hominoid Johanicus—the anthropologists said that he was a direct descendant from Neolithic man and from carbon dating of some clippings from his claws, or nails, depending on which theory you wish to support, must be over one thousand years old."

"As I remember," said Dr Stronberg, "the creature did not survive."

"That's right. Sadly for science, he expired thirty-four days later. We were unable to find a suitable diet which he would eat; but that gave me the clue which led us to increase body fat. By this time I was determined to delve deeper into the possibilities that I saw in prospect of an entirely new field. After years of tests on animals, mostly entirely successful I may add, I was ready for the ultimate test:

"Volunteers were decidedly thin on the ground as you

Americans so amusingly express these things. So in the spirit of science and conviction in the principles for which I was mainly responsible, I decided to become the first human experiment; fortunately I had satisfied myself of the need for additional body fat before I tested the process on myself." Then with a chuckle, he added, "Not so fortunately, I have been unable to part company with this addition as you will have already noticed; I must also tell you that there is a marked increase in mental ability afterwards; it's as though the brain responds and is rejuvenated by the rest! I would remind you that normal sleeping periods are mostly required to rest the brain rather than the body. To my regret now I only arranged for a six-month hibernation for myself. But the risk I took has paid off; once we had established that the process was viable, there was an immediate demand for what was seen as a method of delaying death. The hope is that in the future science will have discovered either immortality or a longer lifespan than we enjoy at the present time. You may be aware that I am the senior consultant for Futurelife Inc; which as you will recall is a commercial corporation entrusted to freeze and store bodies for any given period. Unfortunately we have not yet arrived at the first regeneration time which has been contracted for; no-one wanted a shorter period than one hundred years; but I am confident that some of our customers will achieve a mental stature of genius when they are eventually revived!"

These events were the preliminaries to the mass hibernation programme that was now proceeding; the venturers had drawn lots for time slots in the programme. Ched Taylor with his wife Eva had volunteered to be the first human subjects; this was immediately after the pigs that Paul was so insistent on taking with us. The three Swiss scientists were quick to follow; after this demonstration of confidence in the process, the rest of the colonists resigned themselves to their allotted places.

CHAPTER
TWENTY FIVE

"Have we a recording of the scans that were taken from the time that you were first alerted to this object which is following us?" I asked Anthea.

Anthea quickly replied, "It will take a while to retrieve it, but of course we keep a file that records all instrumentation-function which has taken place since we left Earth. I'll initiate an immediate search; have you noticed that the estimated trajectory is changing?"

I looked over to the screen where the forecast for the following ten hours appeared. "You're right," I exclaimed, "but there's also a time change; it's closing rapidly; it should be within reach of our anti-meteorite lasers at any time!"

Then the significance of what was happening suddenly struck me like a sledgehammer; if this object could change both speed and direction, it must be under control! Anything that could change direction in space millions of light years away from anything other than occasional chunks of space debris must by any stretch of imagination be directed by some intelligence! I stretched across the control console to switch the data which was being fed to the forecast plot onto the giant viewing screen; the picture I looked for was disappointing; a mere point of light, an indication that something had been detected; no outline of shape or size. I was about to speak to Anthea again. I turned towards her; the picture I saw filled me with dismay. Always in my deep subconscious were doubts regarding the ultimate dependability of the Androids. Now I watched in silence as a rigid Anthea stood by the side of the power indicator console; she was gripping the front edge of the flat desk top; her body was perfectly stationary with a vacant look in her eyes, which gazed straight ahead. I remembered Curt telling me once that they had built an automatic blink into the programme for their Androids as this was one of the most noticeable and to humans, disconcerting features of a Robot; there was no need for them to blink and an unblinking eye was very disturbing to the average human. Now, I was experiencing that unease for myself. I watched for almost two minutes before Anthea appeared to recover her normal poise, then she spoke.

"I am being subjected to a scanning process of which I have no understanding, Ro!" A moment later Anthea spoke again, but now her voice took on a different quality; it was no longer the pleasing cultured vibrant tone which we found so attractive; it was a purely mechanical sound, quite understandable but flat and harsh.

"WELCOME; to our mind! We regret that our method of contacting you is so primitive, but until we get to know you more fully, we must exercise a cautious means of addressing you. We felt that we must make contact with you immediately because we are aware that you control a means of disrupting matter which we must forestall. We repeat; we greet you in peace and tranquillity."

I was dumbfounded; what could this mean? My thoughts

raced around in my head. What was this creature or intelligence that managed to exist out here in deep space? Then my mind switched to the object that appeared to be chasing us; was this voice somehow being transmitted from that?

My mind was in turmoil; my throat seemed suddenly to have dried.

"Who are you?" I croaked.

The reply was instant; again through Anthea's lips: "Like you, we are travellers in space; we are looking for fresh interests and stimulation. Would you care to meet us?"

"How can I do that?" I questioned cautiously.

"You must transpose yourself to our vessel. We are anxious to feel what form you are!"

That was a queer statement, I thought; what did they mean by 'feel what form you are'?

Well, I was unable to 'Transpose myself', whatever that may mean; then I wondered if I should invite this alien voice into my ship; presumably the voice was able to accomplish this feat.

I immediately went on to wonder if this would be a prudent step to take. Was it sensible to invite a totally unknown quantity into the ship? This train of thought was interrupted once more.

"We sense that you are uneasy; we repeat that we are fellow travellers; we have no hurtful intentions toward you or your companion; if you will open a communication link we can converse more easily. We are reluctant to communicate with your own intelligence directly; we have no way of knowing what schematics you use and would not wish to project possible harmful vibrations."

This set me a problem; what sort of transmission system

would be in use? To enable penetration through the shielding of our craft must involve extremely short wave-length energy; this would suggest light as the most likely method in use. I switched on the lasercom receiving scanner...

"GREETINGS..." The volume was deafening! I hastily reduced the power level, and then tried the transmitter.

"I greet you. My name is Ro Stern; I am in command of this ship. We are from the planet Earth whose co-ordinates are..." I quickly looked for the details from the Star atlas. I hesitated, "I am afraid that I have not yet located our current position, so that information is not available at present."

"Greetings Ro-stern. We call ourselves 'Allthoughts'. There are many individuals but we share our property and thinking and act in unison. We have been following you for many time units but until just recently because we could detect no signs of life we assumed that you were an exploration craft without intelligence; then suddenly we have detected vibrations. Please explain the reason."

I proceeded to describe how we had been in a state of limbo while our craft journeyed to the star cluster, which had been identified as being a possible area in which to search for a planet on which we hoped to start a new community. While I was speaking I saw that Anthea had returned to her normal condition; when I paused, Allthoughts said:

"We apologise for assuming control of your companion but we found there circuitry which we could understand and chose to make ourselves known to you as quickly as we could. We left our own planet many time periods ago; our star was about to go into a new stage of its progression through its life cycle, which would absorb our planet. Is this the reason why you left your world?" Without waiting for an answer the voice continued.

"When we had been exploring for many time periods, our people gradually started to acclimatise to life on our craft. As generations succeeded each other our form altered; we no longer required limbs with which to manipulate objects; we found how to cause matter to realign into the pattern we desired. We no longer needed to visit each other to communicate, we discovered how to transfer our thoughts to one another by merely thinking; we then discovered that by combining our minds into one whole actuality we could amplify our understanding and all share of the knowledge available to any one member. Once we accepted this way of living the power of our minds increased progressively beyond all imagination. We no longer required a planet on which it would be necessary to endure the elements, we could remain in our comfortable home and travel the universe; explore worlds which were far too distant for one lifetime to reach, but that was no problem; our children or their children could go there and then their children will go somewhere else."

There was a silence; to say that I was astonished would be only a half truth. I was overwhelmed; my mind was so overflowing with suppositions and the wildest thoughts started and were left unfinished because I dared not follow them through, they were too preposterous; if these creatures did not require limbs, what shape would they be? They spoke of feeling: did this mean that they had no eyes? If they lived entirely within a spacecraft there would be nothing to look at; my mind filled with visions of a brain enclosed within a crystal sphere floating inside their vessel—and what was their vessel like? I thought that my brain was about to burst and refuse to function any longer. What manner of beings were these creatures that were talking quite casually about telepathy, telekinesis, and existing permanently in a state of peregrination. I urgently required another person with whom to discuss these extraordinary circumstances; no matter Curt's positive assurances that Anthea was capable of original thought, I could not bring myself to take her into my confidence; I always saw Anthea as an elaborate appliance complete with sexuality programmed into her electronic brain. There was another aspect; these creatures, Allthoughts as they called themselves, could apparently enter Anthea's brain, therefore anything, which I discussed with Anthea, was available to the aliens.

If ever I was in need of my capacity for rapid assimilation of information it was at this time. I preceded to list in my mind the facts that were available. First, we could not run away; the alien ship had already demonstrated how it could increase its speed at will and *Han Venturer* was travelling at its maximum speed now! Fortunately the alien appeared to be benign, but was this a deception? The facts remained, the alien had already detected our laser energy protective screen and presumably was remaining at the limit of its range. I wondered why my first thoughts were suspicious and aggressive; was it not possible that a benign life form could exist in exactly the way that had been described and be entirely candid and trustworthy? I looked towards Anthea. She had a faint smile on her lips; was it possible that she guessed my thoughts? What if the aliens had entered her mind and had extended their power of thought reading to her!

A fresh interruption, more information to assimilate.

"We can sense your bewilderment; we repeat, we have no hurtful intentions: there is so much of wonderment and surprise to discover that we are fully occupied with our voyages through the universe to wish harm to any other life form.

"As a little entertainment for us we have calculated the reverse of your journey and now know from where you came; it may interest you to learn that our forebears visited your planet many time periods ago. Life of an extremely primitive form existed at that time; the exploration is recorded in our archives, and we have included it in our programme for a return visit to see what sort of development has occurred. Obviously from your presence here, that must be considerable."

Notwithstanding my present preoccupations, I smiled as I wondered what the Allthoughts would think of the situation on Earth as it had been when we left! The power seeking, the corruption and the restriction to further enterprise such as space exploration; the sop of unlimited entertainment to bemuse the minds of the masses.

I had left the receiver open. Once more the voice entered the interior of *Han Venturer*. I noted that the voice had modified to a far more agreeable tone. I realised with a start that it sounded like a recording of my own voice; these aliens were certainly quick to copy.

"We understand from Anthea that you are seeking a planet to re-start your lifestyle; you do not wish to return to the place from which you have come."

On at least one point I was satisfied with my decision not to include Anthea in my judgement of how to deal with the dilemma we now faced. I now realised that I must make this decision without help from anyone!

"That is correct—perhaps you can help us?"

"If you wish for our help, ask Anthea to co-operate; the information we have obtained up to the present time has involved us in great effort."

That was some consolation, I thought. I spoke out to Anthea:

"I think that our best course of action will be to accept whatever help is available from the Allthoughts. Anthea, please allow them to explore your memory circuits for whatever information they require."

I stood up from my chair; my back ached, my mind was racing round and round trying to digest the implications of this fresh intelligence. I found it difficult to think at all. I moved to the transmitter. "I need rest," I said, "I must sleep. Anthea will inform you when I waken."

I went over to a cot to rest. I thought, I must consider what I know at present before I try to accept anything more. As my head touched the pillow I fell into a deep sleep as though I was drugged.

I awoke twelve hours later. I was astounded at my feeling of perception and confidence; at the instant of waking I remembered everything of the events which had occurred since my regeneration. I was filled with a degree of excitement and a desire to start on the next stage of this wonderful adventure. I remembered how Professor Shasimoso had forecast increased mental ability as a benefit to be expected from extended resting of the brain.

"Are you rested, Ro?" Anthea enquired in a solicitous voice. I recalled my visit to the Swiss scientists' laboratory when Curt had so passionately declared that they would create an Android the equal of man. The concern apparent in Anthea's voice was a demonstration of their progress. I answered with energy. "I feel fit for anything," and was about to add, "bring on the dancing girls"—when I thought better of it. Instead I asked Anthea if there had been any recent communication with the aliens. Anthea answered calmly. "They have transmitted to me directions which they say will lead us to a planet that is similar to Earth as it existed at the time of their earlier inspection."

"That will be perfect! How far away is it?"

"My calculations estimate it as being a little more than one of our years," was Anthea's reply. "The Allthoughts have left, Ro. They said that they would visit this planet in ten time spans, which I calculate to be approximately one hundred years from now!"

I was considering; this Planet would seem to be exactly what we had set out to search for. It was too soon to regenerate the rest of the community; life on board our vessel would be uncomfortably crowded once they were all out of their cocoons. I brought the external viewing screen to life and gazed into the dark velvet of space with its scattering of brilliant points of light, one of which would surely be the new sun to which we were heading. What would the future hold for me and the four hundred souls that were in my care? Well, I would have ample opportunity to speculate on that. Which left me with about nine months to work on the story about this adventure, which I was determined to chronicle. In between that and catching up with some reading that I had never found time for previously, I would have ample opportunity to find out what sort of companionship Anthea could provide.

I grinned to myself as I realised the direction in which my thoughts were leading me. I turned to look at Anthea with the smile still on my lips. I idly wondered if it would be necessary to exchange the software programme disc; I would need to look up the operating manual.

Anthea automatically updated her profile of human beings.

She noted that this was the first occasion on which Ro Stern had smiled when addressing her.

THE END